ROOTS OF RESISTANCE

A JOURNEY BEYOND THE CROWN

JR

Contents

Contents

PREFACE

In a realm where magic and tyranny intertwine, one young princess dares to defy the expectations placed upon her. Roots Of Resistance: A Journey Beyond The Crown invites you into the enchanting world of Eryndor, where shadows lurk in every corner and hope flickers like a candle in the dark.

At its heart lies Elora, a spirited and determined princess who yearns for freedom—not just for herself, but for the countless souls suffering under the oppressive rule of a dark warlord. As she embarks on a journey through enchanted forests and treacherous mountains, she discovers her own latent powers and the strength of true friendship. Alongside her new allies—Lyra, the fierce and loyal friend, and Ronan, the brooding warrior with a troubled past—Elora learns that courage is not the absence of fear, but the resolve to fight for what is right.

This story weaves together themes of rebellion, self-discovery, and the transformative power of unity. It explores the complexities of trust, the struggles of harnessing one's inner strength, and the delicate balance between light and darkness. As Elora confronts her own demons, she also finds unexpected connections that challenge her understanding of loyalty and love.

Join Elora on her quest as she navigates the harsh realities of her world, faces betrayal and danger, and ultimately rises to become a beacon of hope. Whispers of the Wild is a tale for anyone who has ever felt the call to stand against injustice, to embrace their true selves, and to believe that even in the darkest times, change is possible.

Let the adventure begin.

PROLOGUE

"They are the spark in the darkness, the sword in the silence, and the shield for the forgotten."

Elora: *Elora's journey begins with a deep desire for freedom, not just for herself but for the oppressed people of Eryndor. Despite being a princess, she rebels against the confines of her royal life, secretly training in swordsmanship and mingling with the common folk. Her connection with the villagers and their struggles fuels her determination to stand up against the tyrannical warlord. Elora becomes the leader of a rebellion, driven by a powerful sense of justice and a desire to protect her kingdom from the darkness that looms*

Ronan: *Ronan, a brooding warrior with a mysterious past, plays a pivotal role in the resistance. A seasoned fighter, he is haunted by the losses and battles of his past, yet his strength and strategic mind make him a vital leader. He is initially portrayed as cold and distant, but as he fights alongside Elora, he reveals a deeper, more complex side—a man driven by honor and a desire to protect those he cares about. His relationship with Elora evolves as they navigate the challenges of their rebellion*

<u>Lyra:</u> *Lyra is introduced as a skilled thief and "acquisition expert" who has suffered great personal loss at the hands of the warlord. Behind her sharp wit and mischievous personality lies a tragic story of survival. Lyra fights not just for freedom, but to avenge the destruction of her family and home. Her loyalty to Elora and the cause is unwavering, and she becomes a trusted and valuable ally in their quest to overthrow the warlord*

I

INTRODUCTION TO ERYNDOR

Eryndor, a realm woven from the very fabric of magic, was a kingdom that dazzled the eyes and stirred the soul. The land itself seemed to breathe with an ancient pulse—trees towering like sentinels of old whispered secrets in the wind, and rivers sparkled as if the waters themselves had absorbed the light of the stars. Each corner of the kingdom was a reflection of the magic that flowed through its veins, and the different realms of Eryndor were shaped by the unique powers of the houses that ruled them.

In the towering mountains of House Pyra, flames danced with a will of their own, burning with an almost sentient will that mirrored the fierce and fiery nature of the Pyrian people. The mountains glowed with a soft orange hue as molten rivers of lava carved paths down their rocky slopes. It was said that the

Pyrian forges could craft weapons imbued with magic strong enough to shatter stone and cleave through steel. The people of Pyra lived in harmony with the fire, their mastery over the element passed down through generations.

On the other side of the kingdom, the waters of House Aquara shimmered in a kaleidoscope of blues and greens, calming the spirits of all who ventured near. The lakes, deep and still, were said to hold ancient creatures beneath their serene surfaces—creatures bound to the water by old magic. Here, the people lived in peace, their powers focused on healing and nurturing the natural world around them. The magic of Aquara could soothe even the most troubled of souls, and the lakes were often sought out by those who needed respite from the chaos of the outside world.

At the very heart of Eryndor, however, stood the seat of the most revered house of all: House Aeloria. The castle of Aeloria was a sight to behold, its spires piercing the sky like the aspirations of its people. It was said that the castle itself was alive with magic, its stone walls imbued with spells of protection and vitality. Vines with flowers of every color crept up the towers, blooming even in the coldest winter, a testament to the house's mastery over nature. The castle was both a sanctuary and a fortress, filled with enchanted artifacts that glowed softly in the twilight, their magic a reminder of the kingdom's rich and storied past.

The tapestries that lined the halls of the castle were not ordinary depictions of history—they moved, coming to life to retell the great tales of Eryndor's heroes, battles, and victories. The air within the castle walls was always tinged with the scent of blooming flowers, the sweet aroma carried by the gentle hum of nature's pulse. Guardian spirits, ethereal beings of light and shadow, drifted through the halls, their presence both comforting and mysterious.

The rulers of Aeloria, King Aldrin and Queen Seraphine, were beloved by their people, their reign characterized by wisdom, compassion, and the deep connection they shared with the natural world. The royal family of Aeloria was known for its unique ability to commune with nature spirits—wisps of smoke that whispered ancient secrets, guiding them through difficult decisions and strengthening their rule with wisdom from ages past. Under their rule, the kingdom had flourished, and peace had reigned for many years.

But peace, as Princess Elora was beginning to learn, was fragile.

Elora, the jewel of House Aeloria, had lived her entire life under the watchful gaze of her parents and the kingdom's people. She was adored by all, a symbol of hope and prosperity. Yet, despite the admiration that surrounded her, Elora felt a deep unrest growing within her. Raised to embody grace, dignity, and the responsibility of her lineage, the crown that awaited her felt more like a shackle than an honor.

The walls of the castle, once a place of comfort, had begun to feel like a prison. Her days were filled with the endless cycle of royal duties—attending council meetings, hosting banquets, and smiling for diplomats—all while the weight of expectation bore down on her shoulders. Her parents' dreams for her future, particularly their desire to arrange her marriage to a noble suitor from a distant land, loomed over her like a storm cloud, stifling her adventurous spirit.

Elora longed for freedom. She dreamed of walking beyond the castle grounds, of exploring the vibrant and magical realms of Eryndor without the constraints of her title. The palace gardens, with their lush greenery and enchanted blooms, called to her in quiet moments, their magic a small taste of the world that lay beyond. She often found herself standing at the edge of the gardens, staring out at the distant horizon, wondering what secrets the ancient forests and towering mountains held.

But even as she dreamed of escaping, Elora was acutely aware of the growing discontent in the kingdom. The whispers of rebellion among the common folk had reached her ears, carried by the winds that rustled through the leaves of the castle's trees. The people, once content and prosperous, were beginning to suffer under the weight of oppressive taxes and the cruelty of the warlord who had slowly begun to claim control over

Eryndor's lands.

The evening banquet was a spectacle of splendor, the opulence of the feast a stark contrast to the turmoil stirring beyond the palace walls. As Elora moved through the crowded hall, laughter echoed around her, but it felt hollow. She caught snippets of conversation among the nobles, their chatter tinged with an air of unease. "Have you heard of the warlord's latest demands?" one noble whispered. "The peasants are restless; they say they will no longer pay."

Elora's heart raced as she processed the words. The laughter and merriment around her felt like a thin veneer over the rising tide of unrest. A fleeting thought crossed her mind: was she to be a mere pawn in this game of power, destined to wear a crown while her people suffered?

Despite the cheerful façade she wore, her mind wandered to thoughts of rebellion, of breaking free from the chains that bound her. The crown that awaited her felt heavy, and the path her parents had laid out for her suffocating. As she listened to the sounds of clinking goblets and joyous revelry, a voice within her whispered, Something must change.

As the sun dipped below the horizon, casting the sky in hues of orange and lavender, she made her way to the balcony. The scent of blooming flowers filled the air, mingling with the distant sound of rustling leaves. She *closed her eyes and let the cool breeze wash over her, envisioning the vibrant lands of Eryndor beyond the castle walls.*

In that moment, she made a quiet promise to herself. She would not allow herself to be confined by the expectations of others. The stars began to twinkle overhead, and with each breath, she felt a flicker of determination ignite within her. She would find a way to break free and discover her own path, one that would lead her beyond the castle grounds and into the heart of Eryndor, where the true battle for the kingdom's future would be fought.

With a final glance at the horizon, Elora turned away from the banquet and toward her destiny, ready to embrace whatever lay ahead

II

ELORA'S REBELLION

The life of a princess was not one of freedom, but of duty. Elora had known this for as long as she could remember. From the time she was old enough to walk, her days were filled with lessons on diplomacy, etiquette, and the intricacies of royal governance. And though her parents, King Aldrin and Queen Seraphine, were loving and kind, they had high expectations for her.

"Smile, Elora. A future queen must always appear confident and gracious," her mother would remind her at every banquet, as suitors and nobles lined up to catch a glimpse of the kingdom's treasured princess.

Elora would comply, a perfect smile plastered on her face. But inside, she felt stifled. The walls of the palace, grand and beautiful as they were, felt more like the bars of a cage. She was adored, admired, but never truly free. Her future was not her own—it belonged to the kingdom, to the crown.

One evening, after another long day of royal obligations, Elora stood by the window of her chamber, staring out at the vast expanse of Eryndor. The moon bathed the land in a soft, silver glow, and she longed to be out there, among the forests and hills, far from the constraints of her title.

"Elora, you can't keep doing this to yourself," she muttered under her breath. "You weren't born just to be a pawn in their game."

Determined to reclaim a piece of her life, no matter how small, Elora made a decision. She would rebel, not with words or grand declarations, but with quiet defiance. Each night, when the palace fell silent and the courtiers retired to their chambers, she would slip out of her room and make her way to the eastern courtyard—a part of the castle long forgotten, overgrown with vines and shaded by towering trees.

There, hidden beneath the moonlight, she practiced.

Her weapon of choice was an unassuming sword she had taken from the armory—far from the jeweled blades of ceremony, it was a practical weapon, forged *for real combat. She swung it with growing confidence, her movements clumsy at first but gradually becoming more fluid. Elora had no formal training, but she had spent years watching the guards train in the courtyard. She mimicked their footwork, their stances, learning through observation and sheer determination.*

One night, as she practiced her strikes, she heard a voice behind her.

"You're holding the sword too tight."

Startled, Elora whirled around, her heart pounding in her chest. There, standing at the edge of the courtyard, was Alaric, a grizzled old palace guard who had been with the royal family for decades. His face was lined with age, but his eyes were sharp as ever.

"Alaric!" she gasped, lowering the sword. "I—what are you doing here?"

"I could ask you the same," Alaric replied, stepping into the moonlight. He looked at her, the corners of his mouth quirking into a small smile. "Didn't think I'd find the princess of Eryndor playing with swords at this hour."

Flustered, but she didn't look away. "I'm not playing. I'm practicing."

Alaric raised an eyebrow. "Practicing for what, exactly? Planning to join the royal guard, are we?"

She sheathed the sword and crossed her arms. "Maybe I should. At least then I wouldn't be stuck in endless meetings with old men who care more about treaties than people."

The old guard chuckled. "You've got fire in you, girl. Always did. But you'll hurt yourself if you keep holding that blade like it's a piece of delicate jewelry. You need to let it become an extension of your arm."

Elora hesitated. "Will you show me?"

For a moment, Alaric seemed to consider her request. Then, with a sigh, he stepped forward and took the sword from her hand. "All right, let's see what you've got." He handed it back, adjusting her grip. "Loosen up. The sword is your friend, not your enemy."

They spent the next hour together, Alaric guiding her through the basics—how to balance her weight, how to strike without losing her footing. Elora's heart raced with excitement. This wasn't just practice—it was a taste of freedom, a chance to be something other than the princess who sat on a throne, making decisions that felt hollow.

As the session came to an end, Alaric looked at her with a mixture of pride and concern. "You've got talent, Princess, but sword fighting isn't just about swinging a blade. It's about what you're willing to fight for."

Elora met his gaze, her voice steady. "I know what I'm fighting for."

Her rebellion didn't end there. It grew.

By day, Elora fulfilled her royal duties—attending council meetings, listening to her parents discuss diplomatic strategies, and smiling for foreign dignitaries. But by night, she became someone else. She wasn't just Princess Elora, the jewel of Eryndor. She was a warrior in training, determined to find her own path.

And soon, her rebellion extended beyond the palace walls.

Disguised in a simple cloak, she would sneak out through a secret passage she had discovered as a child, one that led from the palace gardens into the bustling streets of Eryndor. The city was alive with noise and color—vendors calling out their wares, children playing in the streets, the scent of freshly baked bread wafting through the air.

It was here, among the common folk, that Elora truly began to understand the kingdom she was meant to one day rule.

"Fresh bread, Princess!" Jane, a local baker, called out one evening as Elora passed by. Though Jane didn't know her true identity, she had come to recognize Elora's face beneath the cloak. "Come, have a taste. The best in Eryndor, I swear."

Elora smiled and approached the stall, accepting a warm loaf of bread. "I can't resist," she said, breaking off a piece and savoring the flavor. "You weren't lying. This is amazing."

Jane beamed. "I keep telling the nobles, but they're too busy with their fancy feasts to care about simple bread like mine."

Elora's smile faltered slightly, but she said nothing. She knew all too well how disconnected the nobility had become from the lives of the people.

As she walked further through the market, she overheard a group of farmers talking in hushed tones. Their voices were filled with frustration and anger.

"Half my harvest, gone," one man muttered, shaking his head. "How am I supposed to feed my family when the warlord's men take everything?"

"Same here," another added. "They came through our village last week, demanding more taxes. We barely have enough to survive as it is."

Elora's heart sank as she listened. These were her people—the people she was supposed to protect. And yet, the crown, her crown, had done nothing to stop the warlord's tyranny.

She stepped closer, lowering her hood slightly. "Have you tried speaking to the king?" she asked, her voice soft but urgent. "Surely, he can help."

The farmers turned to look at her, their expressions a mix of bitterness and disbelief. "The king?" one scoffed. "He's too busy hosting banquets to care about farmers like us. We're on our own."

Elora felt a pang of guilt. They were right. The crown had been too focused on diplomacy, on maintaining peace with the warlord, to see the suffering of their own people. And she had been complicit in that neglect.

"I'm sorry," she whispered, more to herself than to them. "I didn't know."

The farmers gave her a strange look but said nothing more. As they turned away, Elora stood frozen, the weight of their words heavy on her heart.

That night, as Elora returned to the palace, her mind raced. She could no longer ignore the suffering of her people. She couldn't sit idly by while they were crushed under the warlord's boot. But what could she do? She was just one girl, with no army, no allies, and no real power.

But Elora was not one to give up easily.

"Enough," she whispered to herself as she stood in her chamber, staring out at the darkened kingdom. "I will not be a silent princess. I will fight."

• 15 •

Her rebellion would not be grand, not yet. But it would grow. She would train harder, seek out those who would stand with her, and when the time came, she would lead.

She would not be confined by the expectations of others. Eryndor needed someone to stand up for the people, and if no one else was willing to, then she would.

III

THE HIDDEN VILLAGE

The night air was cool against Elora's skin as she slipped through the palace gates, her cloak wrapped tightly around her to keep her hidden. She had become skilled at sneaking out unnoticed, and tonight, she was more determined than ever to escape the suffocating confines of the palace. Her encounters in the marketplace had stirred something deep within her—a need to do more, to truly understand the world beyond the walls of her royal home.

As she moved silently through the forest beyond the city, her heart raced, not with fear, but with anticipation. The Whispering Woods stretched out before her, its towering trees casting long, dark shadows in the moonlight. The forest was said to be enchanted, a place where ancient magic still lingered, and few dared to venture too deep within its borders.

But Elora wasn't afraid. She welcomed the unknown. Anything was better than the life of idle luxury that awaited her back at the castle.

Her footsteps were light, her senses alert as she ventured deeper into the woods. The forest was alive with the sound of rustling leaves and the distant hoot of an owl. The trees seemed to whisper secrets to one another, their branches swaying gently in the breeze. Elora's pulse quickened. She felt as though the forest was watching her, guiding her toward something she couldn't yet see.

As she pressed on, the path became less defined, the trees thicker and more twisted. Just as she began to wonder if she was truly lost, a faint light flickered through the trees ahead. Elora's breath caught in her throat. She hadn't expected to find anyone this deep in the forest. Curiosity and caution battled within her, but her feet moved forward, drawn toward the light.

As she approached, the outline of a small village began to take shape. It was a far cry from the grand cities she had known all her life. The houses were simple, built from wood and stone, their roofs thatched with straw. The village was nestled in a clearing, hidden away from prying eyes by the thick canopy of trees that surrounded it. A soft mist clung to the ground, giving the entire place an ethereal, almost magical quality.

Elora's heart pounded in her chest as she stepped cautiously toward the village. She had never seen anything like this before—a place so isolated, so untouched by the outside world. But as she moved closer, she noticed something else. The village was eerily quiet. There were no sounds of laughter, no bustling activity. The people here moved slowly, their faces lined with weariness, their eyes downcast.

Just then, a voice called out from the shadows. "Who goes there?"

Elora froze, her hand instinctively moving to the hilt of the dagger hidden beneath her cloak. From the darkness, a figure emerged—a man, tall and broad-shouldered, with sharp eyes that glinted in the dim light. He looked at her with suspicion, his stance tense.

"I—I'm just passing through," Elora stammered, unsure of what to say. She wasn't used to being confronted like this.

The man's eyes narrowed. "No one 'just passes through' the Whispering Woods. Who are you, really?"

Elora hesitated. She could tell by his hardened expression that he wasn't easily fooled. The people in this village weren't like the courtiers back at the palace—they wouldn't be swayed by charm or flattery. Deciding that honesty was her best chance, she slowly pulled back her hood, revealing her face.

"I'm Elora," she said quietly. "Princess Elora, of House Aeloria."

The man's eyes widened in shock, but his expression quickly hardened again. "The princess?" he spat, his voice laced with bitterness. "What's royalty doing this far from the palace? Come to see how the other half lives, have you?"

Elora flinched at his words but stood her ground. "I'm not here to gawk at your suffering," she said, her voice steady. "I'm here because I want to help. I know what the warlord has done to our people, and I can't stand by any longer."

The man crossed his arms, clearly unconvinced. "Help? From a princess? What do you know about our suffering? You live in a palace, surrounded by wealth and power, while we scrape by with nothing. What could you possibly do for us?"

Before Elora could respond, another voice cut through the tension—a softer, but firm voice. "Ronan, that's enough."

From behind the man, an older woman stepped forward. Her hair was streaked with silver, and her face was weathered with age, but her eyes were sharp and intelligent. She studied Elora for a moment before nodding slightly. "Let the girl speak."

Ronan—clearly the man's name—grumbled but stepped aside, his eyes still wary.

Elora took a deep breath and addressed the woman. "I know I'm just one person, and I know I come from a world that's far removed from the suffering you've endured. But I've seen what's happening in Eryndor. I've seen the pain the warlord has caused. I want to fight back, but I can't do it alone."

The older woman's gaze softened slightly, though there was still a glimmer of skepticism in her eyes. "And you think you can help us, do you? A princess who's never known hunger, who's never felt the bite of a sword?"

Elora met her gaze, her voice resolute. "I may not have lived your life, but I'm willing to fight for you. For all of you."

For a moment, there was silence. The villagers had begun to gather, watching the exchange with wary eyes. Ronan still looked unconvinced, but the older woman seemed to be considering Elora's words.

Finally, the woman nodded. "Come," she said. "We'll talk inside."

Elora followed her into a small, dimly lit house. Inside, the air was warm and smelled faintly of herbs. The woman gestured for Elora to sit at a wooden table, while Ronan remained by the door, his arms crossed and his expression still suspicious.

"I'm Mira," the older woman said as she sat across from Elora. "I lead this village. Or what's left of it."

Elora nodded, glancing around at the humble surroundings. "What happened here?"

Mira's face darkened. "The warlord happened. This village used to be prosperous. Farmers, craftsmen, healers. We lived in peace, protected by the magic of the forest. But when the warlord rose to power, everything changed. His men came, demanding taxes, taking what they wanted. Anyone who resisted was killed. Now, we live in hiding, scraping by with what little we have left."

Elora's heart ached at Mira's words. "I had no idea it was this bad."

Mira gave a bitter smile. "How could you? The palace has turned a blind eye to the suffering of the people.

They think their treaties and alliances will keep them safe. But the warlord's reach grows longer every day."

"I don't want to be like them," Elora said quietly. "I don't want to sit in the palace while my people suffer. I want to fight."

Ronan scoffed from his place by the door. "Fight? With what? You think a princess can just stroll in here and lead a rebellion?"

Elora turned to face him, her voice firm. "Maybe I don't have an army, and maybe I don't have the experience you do. But I'm willing to learn. I've been training in secret, and I've seen the people's suffering with my own eyes. I'm not asking you to follow me blindly. I'm asking you to give me a chance."

Ronan narrowed his eyes, but before he could respond, Mira raised a hand. "Enough, Ronan. The girl may be young, but she's not wrong. We need all the help we can get if we're going to survive."

Elora looked at Mira, gratitude swelling in her chest. "Thank you."

Mira nodded slowly. "But understand this, Princess. This isn't a game. People have died fighting the warlord, and more will die before this is over. If you truly want to help us, you need to be prepared for that."

Elora's stomach twisted, but she didn't waver. "I am."

Mira studied her for a long moment, then sighed. "Very well. You can stay. But you'll have to earn your place among us."

"I wouldn't have it any other way," Elora replied, her voice steady.

As her words trailed off, a playful, mischievous voice cut in. "Typical peer pressure from elders eh?"

Elora turned to find the source- a woman not much younger than her, standing with a grin suggested she was no stranger to stirring things up. "Name's Lyra, the life of this- well, not so lively place, also called the equisition expert," she said as she walked towards Elora and takes her hand into a firm yet friendly shake followed by a wink.

Amused more than annoyed by the carefree attitude in such tense situation, Elora accepts the handshake. "Lyra..." she said, her lips curling into a small smirk. "I think..." she paused for a moment enjoying the playful exchange , then added with a touch of humour, "We'll get along just fine."

Lyra's grin widened, her eyes sparkling. "You bet," she replied with infectious enthusiasm as she withdraws her hand.

As Elora stood to leave, Ronan finally spoke, his voice low and filled with warning. "This isn't your world, Princess. You may think you want to fight, but you don't know what that really means. Not yet."

Elora met his gaze, her heart pounding. "Then teach me."

Elora spent the following days in the village, learning more about the people who lived there and the struggles they faced. She helped wherever she could—hauling water, mending roofs, and even tending to the wounded. The villagers were slow to trust her, but over time, they began to see that she wasn't just a pampered princess playing at rebellion. She was serious, and she was willing to fight for them.

Ronan, however, remained distant. Though he grudgingly agreed to train her, he kept her at arm's length, watching her every move with suspicion. Their training sessions were intense, with Ronan pushing her harder than she had ever been pushed before, testing her resolve at every step.

• 25 •

IV
THE PRINCESS'S DILEMMA

As the sun rose the following morning, Elora returned to the palace, her heart heavy with the weight of the villagers' despair. Each step felt like a betrayal as she crossed the threshold into the gilded halls, where laughter and opulence surrounded her, starkly contrasting the suffering she had witnessed. Her mind raced with thoughts of duty, loyalty, and the urgent need for action.

"What are you doing back so soon, Elora?" her father's voice boomed from the throne room, echoing off the marble walls. King Aldrin was seated at the head of a long table, flanked by advisors poring over maps and reports. His brow furrowed, and he looked up with a mixture of concern and annoyance.

"I... needed to discuss something important," Elora replied, her voice steadier than she felt. She stepped closer, determination rising within her as she prepared to voice her thoughts.

"Important? The council is deliberating on how to deal with the warlord's latest demands. You should be focused on your duties, not wandering off," he chastised, his voice sharp.

"I saw the villagers, Father! They're suffering," Elora urged, her heart racing. "They need our help!"

"Help?" he scoffed. "They need to know their place. The warlord's power is not something we can challenge lightly."

"But we must! They are our people, and they're living in fear! How can we stand by while they suffer?" Elora pressed, frustration boiling over.

"You're naive to think we can just confront him," her mother, Queen Seraphine, chimed in softly, concern etched on her face. "The consequences could be dire."

"Consequences?" Elora echoed, her voice rising. "What about the consequences of doing nothing? They are losing hope, and if we don't act, they will lose everything!"

Her parents exchanged glances, their disapproval evident. "Elora, we are trying to maintain peace," the king said, his tone firm. "You must understand the bigger picture."

"The bigger picture?" Elora couldn't hold back her indignation. "It's easy to talk about peace when you're safe behind these walls! I won't sit idly by!"

"Enough!" King Aldrin's voice boomed, silencing her. "You will respect our decisions. This is not a game, Elora. This is politics."

Elora clenched her fists, frustration coursing through her. "Politics? This is about lives! If you won't help them, I will!" She turned on her heel and stormed out of the room, her heart pounding with a mix of anger and determination.

Once alone in her chambers, Elora paced back and forth, the weight of her decision pressing down on her. The kingdom was at a crossroads, and she could no longer hide behind her royal title. Inspired by the strength she had seen in the villagers, she resolved to take action. The warlord's dark magic had to be *challenged, and she would be the one to lead that charge.*

With a quill in hand, she began to scribble her ideas on parchment, her heart racing with urgency. "I need allies," she muttered to herself. "Others who share my vision for a free Eryndor."

She thought of the villagers she had met, their stories echoing in her mind. "I'll seek out those who've experienced the warlord's cruelty firsthand," she whispered. "Together, we can harness the magic of this land and the strength of our people."

But as she prepared to share her plans, doubts crept in. "What if I fail? What if my parents find out?" She took a deep breath, reminding herself of the villagers' faces, their suffering, and the courage she had witnessed. She knew the decision was made; she could no longer remain hidden in the palace.

Elora stormed out of the throne room, anger igniting a fire within her. She would not beg for her father's support any longer. They would not save her people, but she would. Her fingers clenched tightly. "If I am to be a rebel," she whispered fiercely, "then let them see me rise."

That evening, she sneaked out of the palace under the cover of darkness, her heart racing with anticipation.

She made her way back to the hidden village, the flickering stars guiding her path. Upon arriving, she found the villagers gathered around a flickering fire, their faces illuminated by its warm glow.

"Princess Elora!" a young man called out, his voice tinged with surprise and hope. "What brings you back so soon?"

Elora took a deep breath, rallying her thoughts. "I've seen the palace, and I can't ignore your suffering any longer. We need to unite. We can't just react to the warlord's cruelty; we must be proactive."

"What if he finds out?" one villager asked, concern etched on her face. "What if he sends his guards after us again?"

"That's a risk we'll have to take," Elora said firmly. "But I believe if we stand together, we can show him our strength. We can turn fear into courage."

Another villager, a burly man with a weathered face, stepped forward. "I'm with you, princess. We can't keep living like this."

"And we won't!" Elora declared, her voice rising with fervor. "But we need to act quickly. We'll gather everyone who believes in our cause, those willing to

fight back. We'll train, we'll prepare ourselves, and we'll reclaim our freedom!"

As she spoke, the fire crackled, and the villagers exchanged glances, the flicker of hope igniting in their eyes. "What about magic?" the young man asked, a hint of excitement in his voice. "Can we learn to use it against him?"

"Yes!" Elora replied, her heart racing. "There's magic in the land. I believe if we connect with it, we can harness its power to fight back."

One of the older villagers, a woman with silver hair, spoke up. "I know of some ancient rituals that can strengthen our magic," she said. "But it will take time and dedication."

"We have to be willing to put in the effort," Elora said. "This is our chance to change everything. Will you join me?"

One by one, the villagers began to nod, their resolve strengthening. "I'll help however I can," the burly man said. "We'll train, we'll learn, and we'll be ready!"

The young man stepped forward again, determination lighting his eyes. "Count me in. I'll fight for my home and my people!"

"I'll spread the word to the neighboring villages," the silver-haired woman added. "We can gather more supporters."

As the villagers rallied around her, Elora felt a surge of hope wash over her. "Together, we can change our fate," she said, her voice steady. "We won't let fear control us any longer."

Over the next few weeks, they trained tirelessly under the cover of night, the village transforming into a hub of activity. Elora learned to tap into the land's magic, guided by the older villagers who shared their knowledge and wisdom. She practiced the rituals, feeling the energy of the forest flow through her, and watched as hope blossomed in the eyes of her comrades, their spirits lifting with each passing day.

One night, as they gathered around the fire after a long day of training, Elora looked at the faces illuminated by the flames. "I'm proud of all of you," she said, her heart swelling with pride. "We've come so far together, and the strength we've built is just the beginning."

"What if his guards come after us?" the young man asked, anxiety creeping into his voice.

"We're not alone," Elora assured him. "Ronan, the brooding warrior, he's with us, as are his allies. We can use their knowledge of combat to sharpen our skills and plan our strategies."

As the villagers nodded in agreement, a sense of unity filled the air as they took in her assurance. Elora felt a spark of hope igniting within her, a fire that would guide them through the darkness ahead. "We will reclaim our land," she declared. "Together, we will rise!"

The villagers erupted in cheers, their voices echoing through the night. Elora smiled, knowing that she had found her purpose—no longer just a princess, but a leader ready to fight for justice. As the fire crackled and the stars shimmered above, she whispered to herself, "The dawn of a new era is upon us, and I will not falter in my quest for freedom."

V

GATHERING THE STORM

The sun hung low in the sky, casting long shadows over the rugged terrain as Elora and her companions made their way through the dense forest. The air was thick with the earthy scent of damp soil and the sweet fragrance of wildflowers, yet a sense of foreboding loomed like a specter among the trees. Each step felt heavy, weighed down by the enormity of their mission. The rebellion needed allies—people who believed in their cause and were willing to fight against the oppressive regime of the warlord.

As they pushed deeper into the woods, the cacophony of chirping birds and rustling leaves seemed to fade, replaced by the rhythmic pounding of Elora's heart. Doubt crept into her mind like the encroaching darkness. Would they find those who shared their vision? Would they accept her, a royal scorned by her own family, as a leader?

Beside her, Ronan walked with his usual stoic demeanor, his eyes scanning the surroundings with the keen instinct of a seasoned warrior. The sun glinted off the blade of his sword, a constant reminder of the dangers that lay ahead. Elora admired his strength but felt a pang of guilt gnawing at her insides. They were embarking on this journey because of her—because she had refused to bow to the warlord and had chosen to fight for a better world.

"Ronan," she ventured, breaking the heavy silence that had enveloped them. "Do you think we'll find anyone willing to join our cause?"

He glanced at her, his expression unreadable, then returned his gaze to the path ahead. "There are always those who yearn for change, Princess," he replied, his voice steady yet cautious. "But finding them? That's the challenge. The warlord's grip on these lands is suffocating. Fear keeps many silent."

Elora nodded, swallowing hard. "I understand that fear, but we have to inspire them. We need to show them that hope is not lost."

Lyra, who had been walking slightly ahead, turned back to them, her eyes bright with determination. "We will find allies, Elora. I know we will. There are *villages that suffer under the warlord's rule, and they will see the strength in our unity. They'll recognize that they are not alone."*

Her words ignited a spark of hope within Elora, but it was quickly overshadowed by the memories of the fear and despair she had witnessed in her travels. The villages she had seen burned to the ground, the families torn apart by violence—how could she stand before these people and ask them to risk everything for a rebellion that might fail?

"Keep your spirits high, Elora," Ronan said, his voice softer now. "We're on the right path. We just need to remain vigilant. Trust in your conviction."

With renewed resolve, Elora pushed aside her worries, determined to focus on the task at hand. As they continued, the forest began to thin, revealing a clearing where the remnants of a small village lay nestled among the trees. The sun bathed the scene in a golden light, yet the joy of the moment was overshadowed by the palpable tension that seemed to linger in the air.

The village was eerily quiet. Elora could sense the despondency that hung over the place like a heavy cloak. As they approached the first few houses, she saw a group of villagers gathered around what appeared to be a makeshift market, their faces etched with worry and exhaustion.

Elora stepped forward, her heart racing as she approached the villagers. "We come in peace," she called out, her voice strong despite the quivering in her chest. "We are here to help."

The villagers turned to face her, their expressions a mix of curiosity and skepticism. A man with grizzled features stepped forward, arms crossed over his chest, his brow furrowed in suspicion. "What help can you offer?" he demanded, his voice rough and weary. "We've seen nothing but pain from those who come in the name of freedom."

Elora met his gaze, determined to convey her sincerity. "I am Elora, daughter of King Aldrin. I have witnessed the devastation that the warlord has wrought upon this land. I refuse to stand idly by while our people suffer."

A murmur rippled through the crowd, and Ronan stepped forward, positioning himself slightly behind Elora, ready to protect her if necessary. "We seek allies to rise against the warlord," he added, his tone commanding yet respectful. "You are not alone in this fight."

The man narrowed his eyes, skepticism still etched across his features. "Your father has betrayed us, Princess. Why should we trust you?"

Elora's heart sank at his words, but she stood firm, willing to bear the weight of her family's legacy. "I am not my father. I seek to rectify the wrongs he has committed against our people. I believe that together, we can bring about change."

Lyra stepped forward, her voice ringing with fervor. "We've faced great trials, but we've also seen the power of unity. Together, we can reclaim our homes, our families, and our lives."

The crowd exchanged uneasy glances, the seeds of doubt still embedded deep within their hearts. Elora could feel the tension mounting, and she knew she had to act quickly to sway them. "I understand your fear. I've felt it myself. But if we do nothing, we are ensuring our own demise. We must fight for a better future."

The man's gaze softened, a flicker of hope igniting in his eyes. "And if we fight and fall? What then?"

"Then we will have fought with honor," Ronan said, his voice steady, infused with unwavering strength. "But we cannot let fear dictate our lives any longer. Will you join us?"

Elora watched as the man wrestled with his thoughts, the weight of their situation bearing down on him. After a moment, he sighed deeply and turned to the crowd, raising his arms in a gesture of unity. "If we are to stand against the warlord, we must do it together. I will join you, Elora. We will gather our strength and fight."

A ripple of agreement spread through the villagers, and Elora felt a surge of hope wash over her. One by one, they stepped forward, their voices rising in unison as they pledged their allegiance to the cause.

As the sun dipped below the horizon, casting a warm glow across the clearing, Elora felt the beginnings of a new alliance take shape. They were not just gathering allies; they were igniting a flame of hope that had long been snuffed out. The rebellion was growing stronger, and with each step, she felt the weight of her burden lighten.

Elora knew that this was just the beginning. As they stood united in the fading light, she could almost hear the distant rumble of thunder, heralding the storm of change that was about to sweep across Eryndor.

VI
THE GROVE OF SHADOWS

The night pressed in on them, thick with a kind of ancient weight, as if the forest itself was aware of their trespass. The trees loomed, their trunks like dark, silent sentinels, their branches reaching out like skeletal hands to block the moonlight. The air was thick with the scent of wet earth, the dampness of rotting leaves, and something else—a faint, almost imperceptible tang of decay.

Elora's steps were light, careful, but even as she moved, her senses were stretched tight, as though the forest was drawing her in, waiting for some moment to reveal itself. Her heart beat hard against her chest, a constant drum that echoed in her ears. Something was wrong. She had been feeling it for days, but now it clung to the very air around them, curling into the edges of her thoughts like a shadow she couldn't escape.

Ronan moved ahead, his figure a faint silhouette against the sliver of moonlight, each step deliberate, controlled. He was a hunter, she thought, always the one who led them into danger without hesitation, without looking back. His face was hidden by the shadows, but she could feel the weight of his presence.

She followed, her breath shallow, every part of her on edge. It wasn't just the forest; it was him—Ronan, the one who never showed doubt, who never asked questions. It unsettled her. She couldn't decide if his certainty was a strength or a mask.

Lyra, ever the firebrand, moved alongside her, her gaze flicking between the shadows, her hand never far from her blade. "You really think they'll join us?" she asked, voice barely above a whisper, as if speaking louder might shatter the fragile calm of the night.

Elora's gaze flicked to Lyra, her gut tightening with the question. She wanted to be certain, wanted to believe it. But that gnawing doubt—sharp and persistent—kept cutting through every thought. "I have to believe they will," she said, her voice low. The words tasted bitter, as if she was trying to convince herself as much as Lyra. "We can't take on the warlord alone."

Lyra's mouth twisted, a bitter curl of her lips. She didn't need to say what they both knew—how hard it was to ask for help, how much they had fought against those rogue factions in the past. "You think they'll just lay down their arms because you ask? You really think that?"

Elora's fingers tightened around the hilt of her dagger. The cold steel was a comfort, a reminder of what was ahead. "We don't need their trust—not at first. We need them to see we're not a threat. If we can show them we can fight, we can survive, we can unite. Together, we can take him down."

Lyra was quiet for a moment, the air between them thick with unspoken thoughts. Elora could feel the hesitation in her, the fear she was trying to swallow down. She understood it. But it didn't change anything. "If we don't try," Elora said, forcing the words out, "we'll never know. And we don't have a choice."

The forest seemed to press in on them then, its silence deafening. Each step felt heavier, the ground beneath their feet more uncertain, as though they were being *led into some kind of trap. But they couldn't afford to stop. Not now. Not when they were so close.*

And then, ahead of them, the trees parted, revealing a clearing bathed in the eerie glow of moonlight. At its center stood an ancient stone altar, its surface overgrown with moss, the carvings worn and faint. Elora's breath caught as she stepped into the clearing, the weight of the place settling on her chest. It wasn't just an altar; it was a place that had once held power, a power that had since been twisted, corrupted. The air hummed with it, an energy that made her skin crawl.

Ronan stopped short, raising a hand to signal them to halt. His body was rigid, his eyes scanning the clearing with a sharp, calculating gaze. "This place is dangerous," he said quietly. "Stay alert. We don't know what we'll face here."

Elora nodded, her senses stretched thin. Every instinct screamed at her to turn back, to leave this cursed place behind. But they couldn't. Not now.

The rustle of leaves broke the silence, and every muscle in Elora's body tensed, her hand sliding instinctively to the dagger at her belt. She glanced at Ronan—his posture was still, his eyes narrowed in concentration. Lyra was already reaching for her sword, the grip tight, her stance ready for whatever might come.

From the shadows, a figure emerged, moving with a fluid, unnerving grace. They were cloaked and hooded, their form indistinct in the dim light, but the presence was undeniable—a quiet power, ancient and heavy, that made the air feel even thicker. The figure's voice was deep, resonating in the stillness. "Who dares enter the sacred ground of the Eryndorn Circle?"

Elora took a step forward, her hand half-raised in a gesture of peace. Her voice was steady, though inside, her heart raced. "We come seeking allies," she said, forcing the words out despite the tightness in her throat. "The warlord threatens everything we hold dear. We believe that, together, we can stand against him."

The figure's eyes gleamed beneath the hood, calculating, searching. Then, slowly, the hood fell back, revealing a woman's face—sharp, angular, her eyes fierce with a defiance that seemed to pierce through the night. There was power in her presence, raw and palpable, something that made Elora's pulse quicken, though she couldn't tell if it was fear or awe.

"You seek to unite the factions?" The woman's voice was skeptical, tinged with disbelief, as though the idea was so foreign it didn't even warrant serious consideration. "Do you truly believe those who have fought so fiercely for themselves will simply lay down their arms and follow you? Especially you—outsiders, rebels who have come at their heels for so long?"

Elora felt a knot tighten in her chest. She didn't want to say the words again, but they came out anyway, forced through the thickness in her throat. "We don't seek power for ourselves. We seek balance. The warlord's cruelty has torn our land apart. If we don't stand together, we will all fall."

The woman's eyes narrowed, studying her with an intensity that made Elora feel as though she were being weighed—measured, judged. Finally, she spoke, her words like a sentence, final and without mercy. "Words are meaningless. You will need more than conviction to unite the factions. You will need to prove you're worth their allegiance."

Elora's breath hitched, but before she could speak, Lyra stepped forward, her posture rigid with something Elora couldn't quite place. A fire, a desperation, a challenge. "Then we'll prove ourselves," Lyra said, her voice sharp, raw with something deeper than just defiance. "If they need to see strength, we'll show them. We're willing to do whatever it takes."

There was a flicker in the woman's eyes—something unreadable. She studied Lyra for a long moment, her gaze searching, before nodding once. "If you wish to prove yourselves, you must face the trials of the Grove of Shadows. Only then will they see your true strength."

Elora's breath caught. The Grove of Shadows. The name alone made the hairs on the back of her neck stand on end. But she didn't hesitate. There was no room for doubt now. "We accept," she said, her voice steady despite the tremor of fear that ran through her. "Whatever you throw at us, we'll face it."

The woman's expression softened ever so slightly, but there was no comfort in it—only a quiet acknowledgment. With a swift motion, she turned and started walking, her figure disappearing into the darkness. Without a word, they followed.

The deeper they went, the heavier the air became, pressing against their skin like a physical force. The trees grew taller, more twisted, their branches intertwining above them, blocking out what little moonlight there was left. The path narrowed, and every step felt like it was pulling them further into the heart of something ancient, forgotten. Elora's chest tightened with a growing sense of dread, but she forced herself to keep moving.

When they reached the Grove of Shadows, the world around them shifted. The air turned cold—unnaturally cold, seeping into their bones. The shadows in the grove seemed to move, writhing like living things, swirling with whispers that tickled the edges of Elora's hearing. She could feel them pressing in, suffocating. The trees bent unnaturally, their trunks blackened, roots exposed, the ground shifting like it was alive.

"What is this place?" Lyra whispered, her voice barely audible over the sound of the whispering shadows.

"It is a realm of your own making," the woman's voice answered, low and cold, almost drowned out by the overwhelming silence of the grove. "Each shadow here is a reflection of your deepest fears. If you wish to prove your strength, you must face them."

Ronan's breath was shallow as he stared into the swirling darkness. "What kind of trial is this?"

Elora didn't wait for the woman's response. She stepped forward, her heart pounding in her chest as the shadows seemed to reach for her. She could feel them pulling at her, the darkness threatening to swallow her whole.

The Grove of Shadows was no ordinary place. It was a mirror. And it was about to show them everything they had ever feared.

The shadows thickened as Elora pressed deeper into the gloom, each step carrying her further into the clutches of something too real to ignore. The air hung heavy, stifling her with its oppressive weight, while the crushing pressure of her own thoughts closed in, suffocating her from within.

It's too much. I can't do it. The doubt had been gnawing at her for weeks, an unrelenting ache that wouldn't ease. But now, it surged like a tidal wave, overwhelming her.

Then, ahead, the darkness parted. And there they were—her parents, the King and Queen—seated on their thrones. But their eyes were hollow, their faces gaunt, ravaged by some unseen sorrow. The once-grand throne room had decayed, the walls cracked and blackened with soot, as though the warlord's soldiers had marched through, leaving nothing but destruction in their wake.

Elora froze, unable to look away.

Her father, whose regal presence had once commanded entire armies, now appeared a broken man. His eyes, once proud, were filled with nothing but bitter disappointment. His voice echoed through the throne room, thick with regret. "You should have listened to us, Elora," he said, the weight of his words striking her like a blow. "You should have stayed out of it. Look what you've done. Look at what you've cost us. The kingdom is crumbling, and your rebellion... it's only made it worse."

The bitterness in his tone cut through her, and a vise of guilt tightened around her chest. She could see it now—the palace, once vibrant and full of life, was reduced to ruins. The streets outside teemed with the warlord's soldiers, the people starving, suffering. The distant cries of the lost and dying reached her ears, a symphony of despair.

Her mother's voice joined his, softer, laden with sorrow, but no less damning. "You were our hope, Elora. We raised you to lead, to protect this kingdom. But now..." Her voice faltered. "Now you've led it to its grave."

The shadows around her began to twist, shifting like smoke. The throne room vanished, and Elora found herself standing amidst the rubble of the kingdom's capital. The city, once full of life and laughter, was now a ghost town—its buildings shattered, its streets empty, save for the bodies of the fallen. People she had fought beside, friends she had cherished, lay scattered in the dirt, their faces frozen in fear and pain.

Elora stumbled forward, her heart pounding in her chest. This isn't real. It's just a shadow. It's just a shadow.

But it felt too real. The ground beneath her feet hummed with the weight of destruction. The ruin was hers to bear. She could hear her father's voice again, biting and cold, cutting through the silence like a whip.

"You failed them. All of them."

Her breath quickened, panic tightening around her chest. She staggered toward her parents, desperate for them to look at her, to say something, anything, that would absolve her. But they didn't see her. Their eyes were empty, fixed on nothing.

Her mother's voice rose again, more distant now, yet still sharp enough to pierce her soul. "If you had only listened. If you had only stayed out of it, none of this would have happened. This is your fault, Elora. Your rebellion, your defiance. You've cost us everything."

"No," Elora gasped, her words faltering, raw. "No... this isn't me. This isn't what I wanted—"

But her parents remained silent, their faces unchanged, their gaze unwavering and empty.

Her knees buckled beneath her, the weight of the scene pressing down like a thousand stones. She sank to the ground, the cold dirt beneath her palms a stark contrast to the burning ache in her chest. The world seemed to close in, the ruin of her kingdom, the faces of the dead, the guilt, all closing around her in a suffocating grip.

I should have listened. I should have stayed out of it.

The words echoed through her mind, a relentless refrain. She could feel herself drowning in them, the weight of failure dragging her under. This was how it ends.

Suddenly, her mother's voice rose again, sharper than before, cruel in its clarity. "You couldn't save us. You couldn't save anyone."

The words hit her like a dagger, slicing through the last remnants of her resolve.

Elora's vision blurred, her heart pounding, her breaths ragged and shallow. She could feel herself unraveling. She had failed. She had failed everyone. There was no coming back from this. The rebellion had already crumbled before it had ever begun.

Trembling, her fingers brushed the dagger at her belt, its cold metal a familiar comfort—but it wasn't enough. Nothing was enough.

"I couldn't protect anyone," she whispered, her voice barely audible, choked with despair. The thought crushed her. She was sinking too far, too deep. She had lost everything.

Then, a flicker. A spark in the darkness. A whisper—so faint, so distant, that at first she wasn't sure it was real.

It wasn't her mother's voice. It wasn't her father's. It was a thought. A memory, long buried, almost forgotten in the weight of her despair.

The darkness seemed to pulse with a life of its own, as if it were waiting, patient and eager, for something to break. Ronan's boots crunched softly against the dead leaves, but with each step, the air grew heavier, the silence pressing in like a weight on his chest. He had faced countless battles, each more dangerous than the last, yet none of them compared to the tension in this place—the feeling that something was about to happen, something he couldn't escape.

The hairs on the back of his neck prickled. He couldn't shake the sense that something was wrong. The shadows were too thick. The silence too profound. His grip tightened around the hilt of his sword, every instinct warning him to turn back.

But then—there it was.

A flicker of light. A small flame, just beyond the treeline. It caught his eye, and for a moment, it seemed too real—too familiar. The crackling sound followed, distant but unmistakable: the dry, sharp pop of wood burning.

No. Not this.

Ronan's body went cold, and his heart raced. He didn't want to look, but his eyes betrayed him, pulling him toward the flames. The shadows around him twisted, the air thickening, and suddenly, the world shifted.

The light grew brighter, larger, until he was standing there—frozen—outside his childhood home, smoke and fire swirling around him.

The house that had once been filled with warmth, with laughter, was now engulfed in flames. The fire climbed up the walls, crackling and roaring like a living beast, devouring everything in its path. He could hear the desperate shouts of his family from within, but they were muffled, distorted, as though coming from a world far removed from his own.

His chest tightened, his breath shallow, as he stepped forward, his legs heavy with dread. No. This can't be real.

"Mom! Dad!" Ronan's voice cracked, desperate, but there was no answer. His feet felt like they were glued to the ground, his body unwilling to move, while the fire spread, consuming the home he had once known.

He tried to run, but his legs were unresponsive, each step feeling like it came with a cost. Then—there it was. A voice. His father's voice.

"Ronan!"

His heart skipped. He turned, but his father wasn't there. The house burned. Everything was burning. He tried to move, to reach them, but the flames held him back—a wall of fire, impossible to cross.

And then, from the smoke, his father appeared. His silhouette framed by the inferno, his face pale, stricken with fear, but there was something else—something Ronan couldn't place. The smoke swirled around his father's form as his voice echoed again, sharper now, cutting through the crackling fire.

"You weren't there. You weren't there when we needed you."

Ronan's breath hitched. The words slammed into him like a physical blow. He staggered back, his heart pounding in his chest. His father's face, once full of pride, was now twisted with disappointment.

"You failed us."

"No," Ronan whispered, shaking his head violently. "No, I tried. I tried to save you."

But the flames only grew hotter. The smoke thickened, swallowing him whole, and before he could say another word, the vision of his father was replaced by his mother. Her face, just as pale, just as broken, filled his vision. Her mouth moved, her eyes wide with fear, but no sound came out.

"Why didn't you come for us?" her lips seemed to form. The question was clear, unspoken yet haunting.

"Mom... I couldn't... I couldn't get to you..." Ronan's voice cracked, a sob breaking free as he dropped to his knees, reaching out through the smoke, through the fire, but it was too late. He had failed them.

The fire roared, the shadows twisted, pulling him deeper into the nightmare. And then—another figure. His younger sister. Clutching her stuffed toy, her tiny face stained with tears. Her voice echoed in the smoke.

"Ronan... help me..."

He reached for her, but the fire surrounded her, obscuring her from his view. The flames devoured her. And with her, any chance of saving her.

"NO!" Ronan screamed, throwing himself forward, his arms reaching out in vain, but the fire surged, swallowing everything in its path.

His sword was in his hand now, his knuckles white with tension, his body shaking as the memory ripped through him. But he couldn't fight the flames. Couldn't stop the vision. It was too real. Too cruel.

"You weren't there. You couldn't save us." His father's voice, colder this time. You couldn't save us.

Tears burned in Ronan's eyes, his vision blurring, but he forced himself to focus. He couldn't break. He wouldn't.

"Stop!" His voice was hoarse, raw with emotion, but the words caught in his throat. "I—" The flames grew hotter, the memory pressing harder against him. The guilt. The failure. The crushing weight of it all. I should have saved them.

ॐ

As for Lyra....the air felt colder now, as if the darkness had turned from oppressive to suffocating. The air was thick with the weight of what was about to unfold. Lyra's chest tightened as the shadows whispered, as though they were calling to her, pulling her deeper into their embrace. She had already seen the fire that consumed Ronan's family, but what was waiting for her? What shape would her fear take?

She took a step forward, the crunch of leaves beneath her boots louder than ever. But then—the sound. It came from behind her, faint at first, but growing louder. The soft murmurs of laughter, voices blending together in a chorus of familiarity, of home. Her heart skipped, a strange mix of dread and yearning filling her chest.

"No," Lyra whispered to herself, her hand instinctively reaching for her blade. Her body tensed, but she couldn't look away from the shadows that seemed to form in the periphery of her vision. The laughter was joined by the sound of running feet—children's feet, small, light, full of joy. They were running through the fields, weaving between the houses. Her heart clenched.

The village. It was the village she had grown up in—the place that had been her family, the home that had given her a sense of belonging she hadn't even realized she'd needed.

As the laughter grew louder, the shadows took form, slowly shaping into images she couldn't push away. Lyra stood frozen as she saw the village, vivid and bright. Children were playing in the fields, adults gathered around the market square, their faces filled with warmth, smiles stretching across the sunlit faces of the people who had once been her family.

The village was alive with light, joy, and love—exactly as it had been before the warlord's soldiers came.

She saw herself among them, laughing with the children, running alongside them as they played. This was home—the place where she was loved. She could see the faces of those who had taken her in, the adults who had protected her when she had no one else. They were family. She hadn't been just an orphan; she had been one of them.

Her throat tightened as she watched her younger self, smiling and running, the carefree life she had once had. It all seemed so perfect, so real.

And then—the soldiers appeared.

They came like a storm, marching down the narrow streets, their armor glinting in the sunlight. The sound of boots on cobblestones was unmistakable, and then the screams followed. Lyra froze as the scene began to blur and twist. It was as though she was being pulled deeper into the memory, the brightness of her past dimming under the shadows of the warlord's wrath.

"Lyra! Run! Get out of here!" a voice shouted, and Lyra's head snapped to see one of the women from the village, a figure she had known all her life, her face filled with terror. She was standing in front of the children, shoving them toward safety.

"Go! Run!"

The soldiers were already marching toward the village square. They were already spreading out, weapons drawn, and the village—her family—was collapsing around her.

Lyra's legs felt like lead, her feet frozen to the earth, but she had to run. She had no choice. Her eyes scanned the chaos, looking for any way to fight back, but there was nothing. She wasn't strong enough, not alone.

"Lyra, you have to go! They'll kill you if you don't run!"

But she couldn't move. She couldn't leave them. Not like this.

And then, through the smoke and dust, she saw him. The warlord. He stood at the edge of the village, *watching the chaos unfold with cruel amusement. His soldiers tore through the streets, burning homes, slaughtering anyone who resisted.*

The blood. The screams. The cries of children, the shrill sound of panic filling the air, but still, he didn't move.

"Run!" the voice of the woman screamed again, pulling Lyra out of her daze. "Go!"

Lyra tried to move, to fight, but her feet wouldn't obey. She couldn't leave them. Not like this.

But the soldiers were closing in. The village was burning. Her home, her family—her whole world was being torn apart.

"Please," she whispered to herself, as her eyes locked on the woman who had taken her hand when she was small, who had held her when she cried. The woman's eyes were wide, pleading. "Please, you have to go!"

The reality of the moment hit Lyra like a fist to the gut. She couldn't save them. She couldn't save them.

And then, everything shattered.

The vision of the village, the people, her family—it all crumbled into ash, into smoke, into nothing. The warlord's soldiers overtook the square. There was nothing left but flames, screams, and the crushing weight of the loss.

"No..." Lyra's breath came in ragged gasps as the vision began to distort, her younger self standing frozen at the edge of the village, watching the people who had loved her burn.

And then—she was alone.

The shadows in the Grove of Shadows shifted again, this time swirling around her like a storm, pressing in from every side. The laughter of children, the voices of the people she had loved, faded into nothingness. The only thing left was the warlord's soldiers, their faces twisted with cruelty, their laughter echoing in her ears. They were coming for her now.

Lyra's knees buckled, and she fell to the ground, gasping for air. Her hands were shaking. Her pulse pounded in her ears. She could feel the heat of the fire on her skin, the suffocating smoke choking her. She had failed them. She had been too weak, too scared, and now everyone she had ever known was lost forever.

The shadows that had once seemed all-encompassing began to thin, retreating into the undergrowth like fading wisps. The oppressive weight that had gripped Elora, Ronan, and Lyra started to lift, but the silence remained. It was the silence after the storm—heavy with reflection, with lingering unease, but also a sense of release.

Elora was the first to straighten herself, blinking as the darkness that had pressed in on her lifted. Her parents—her fear of seeing them as enemies, as pawns to the warlord—had receded. The harsh whispers of their taunts were quiet now, their accusations fading into the background.

She let out a slow breath, her chest aching with the memory of the haunting image, but she didn't allow it to control her. She had chosen this path. She would see it through.

As she turned toward the others, her eyes found Ronan, still crouched on the ground, his breath ragged. The remnants of his vision—the fire, his family, the suffocating loss—still seemed to weigh on him. But there was something different now in his posture, something that had shifted, an acceptance of his grief that had been missing before.

"Ronan," Elora's voice was soft, but it carried through the stillness. She knelt beside him, but she didn't touch him yet. She understood—sometimes, it was just about letting someone come to terms with their own pain. Slowly, Ronan lifted his head, meeting her eyes.

His face was pale, his expression still haunted, but there was something in his gaze—a flicker of the man who had already moved past his past in so many ways. He was still here. He had survived. He was still fighting, fingers, still trembling, tightened around the hilt of his sword. There were no words, but his eyes softened just a little, as if the crushing weight of the accusation had finally loosened its grip.

From a few steps away, Lyra stood motionless, her eyes still locked on the space where her vision had been. The village, her people, her family—all taken by the warlord. Her entire life, gone in an instant, reduced to smoke and ash.

She had faced it—seen the fire consume the life she had known. Yet now, standing in the Grove, she was still breathing, still standing. The terror had subsided, but the ache—the gnawing emptiness that had followed her for so long—was still there.

"Lyra," Elora said softly, her eyes filled with something warmer than the darkness surrounding them. She approached cautiously, as if waiting for Lyra to decide if she wanted the comfort.

The two locked eyes, and Lyra swallowed hard, her throat tight. Elora stepped forward, and without a word, pulled her into an embrace.

The contact was immediate, soothing. Lyra's breath hitched, her shoulders trembling as the tears that had threatened to break free finally did. She hadn't realized how much she needed this—needed someone who understood.

"Shh," Elora murmured, her voice a quiet hum, steady and comforting as the tension slowly left Lyra's body. "You're not alone. Not now. Not anymore."

Lyra clung to her, and for a long moment, that was all they shared—no words, just the quiet assurance of shared strength. Lyra, for the first time in so long, allowed herself to feel the weight of her past, but without the suffocating fear that had kept her locked inside it for so long.

Elora's grip tightened, her warmth, her presence offering something Lyra had almost forgotten: safety.

But just as she pulled back to look at Lyra, Elora saw Ronan, still sitting apart from them, his gaze far away, as if lost in thought. Lyra, still breathing a little shakily, turned and followed Elora's gaze, and without a word, they both moved toward him.

Ronan was still staring at the spot where the fire had consumed his home, his mind clearly adrift in a memory that hadn't faded, not fully. But as Elora and Lyra approached, he turned to them. The remnants of the boy he had been—the one who had lost so much—were still there in his eyes. But now, there was a flicker of something new. A quiet strength. A recognition that he was no longer bound by his past. He had let it go, or at least, was learning to.

Lyra reached out first. She didn't speak, but placed her hand on his shoulder. It was a simple gesture, but one that conveyed everything she couldn't put into words. She understood his grief because she had lived through it herself.

Elora knelt beside him, her gaze steady. "We fight together. No one stands alone."

The words seemed to anchor them both, the tension between them easing. Ronan's gaze flickered between the two women, and for the first time since they had entered the Grove, he offered them a small, worn smile. It was faint, but it was there—a promise of hope, of renewal.

He nodded quietly.

Elora gave him a small nod, and with that, the three of them stood, side by side, in the midst of the Grove of Shadows, the weight of their pasts still heavy but no longer suffocating. They had faced the ghosts of their pasts and survived.

The shadows that had once clung to them now seemed more distant. It was as if the fear itself had been vanquished, not just by force but by their shared strength, their bond.

The woman awaited them at the edge of the grove, her expression one of approval. "You have faced your fears and emerged stronger...go forth, our people will join you in the battle"

Elora stepped back, her arm brushing Lyra's as she did. Her eyes met Lyra's, then Ronan's. "Let's move forward," she said, her voice steady, filled with a quiet confidence.

They were ready.

And for the first time in a long while, Elora allowed herself to believe it. They were more than ready.

VII
ECHOES OF THE PAST

The fire crackled softly in the darkness, its flames dancing like ghosts, casting long shadows that stretched and morphed into enigmatic shapes across the clearing where Ronan sat. He methodically sharpened his blade, the rhythmic sound of metal against stone slicing through the stillness of the night. Each resounding stroke felt like a heartbeat, echoing in the quiet as if the forest itself held its breath, waiting for something momentous to unfold.

Elora watched him from a distance, her heart heavy with unspoken questions that hung between them like a fog. Ronan had always been a man of few words, a stoic warrior forged in the fires of battle. But recently, his silence had deepened, creating a chasm that pulled him further away. She could sense something lurking inside him, a burden too heavy to share.

Lyra, seated a little further along the fire's edge, stared into the flames, her hands resting on her knees, her mind still heavy with the loss of her village. She didn't often speak, but the quiet tension around her felt as thick as the silence between Ronan and Elora. She, too, had been touched by the shadow of grief. It had marked her in ways she sometimes wasn't sure she could even articulate.

Elora caught Lyra's eye, offering a small nod, an unspoken invitation to join them in what felt like an inevitable conversation. With a slow sigh, Lyra pushed herself to her feet and walked over, her movements measured but deliberate. She could sense that Ronan was slipping into a darker place, and despite her own burdens, she understood the need to draw him out.

"You're quiet tonight," Elora ventured, her voice breaking the stillness as she approached the fire. She settled down across from him, her gaze intent on his sculpted features, searching for the man beneath the armor.

Ronan didn't look up; his hand continued its steady rhythm, the edge of the blade catching the flickering light of the fire. "Sometimes silence is all there is," he muttered, eyes focused on his work, a sentinel sharpening an instrument of war.

Elora tilted her head, studying his face, the shadows pooling beneath his eyes. "You carry so much inside you, Ronan. I can see it. Why won't you let anyone in?"

Ronan's movements stilled for a heartbeat, the weight of her question hanging in the air. Slowly, he resumed sharpening the blade, his expression fixed in an inscrutable mask. For a moment, Elora feared he might rise and retreat into the shadows, as he often did when conversations turned too personal. But this time, he remained, the tension in his shoulders softening just enough to hint at vulnerability.

At that moment, Lyra sat down beside Elora, her presence quiet but unmistakable. She said nothing at first, but her dark eyes watched Ronan with a look of understanding that few could offer. She had seen him fight, seen him burn with rage—but she had also seen the quiet moments that followed, the ones when he thought no one was watching. It was then that his walls crumbled, even if only for a heartbeat.

Ronan's mind drifted back to memories that had long haunted him, memories that had become part of his very being. He could still see his mother's face, feel the warmth of her touch before the flames took her away. Her soft voice singing him to sleep, the way her laughter filled their small home, all of it ripped away in an instant by the warlord's men. He swallowed, pushing back the pain that threatened to spill over. That loss had become a shield—a barrier he'd built around himself. He couldn't risk losing anyone like that again.

"Because once you open that door, it never closes," he finally replied, his voice low, layered with unspoken pain. The admission hung in the air, a fragile truth trembling on the edge of revelation.

Elora frowned, confusion swirling in her mind like leaves caught in a storm. "Maybe that's the point. Maybe you're supposed to let others carry the burden with you."

Lyra, whose gaze had been on the fire, looked at Elora then Ronan, and spoke softly, but with quiet authority. "Sometimes we don't get the choice to carry the burden alone. It follows you, even when you think it won't." Her voice was calm but edged with the rawness of her own grief. "You can try to lock it away, but the darkness doesn't just leave."

Ronan met Lyra's gaze, and for a moment, the soldier faded, revealing a man haunted by specters of his past—memories too painful to recount. "I wasn't always like this. There was a time when I believed in more than just war." His voice trembled, a delicate thread woven with sorrow.

He turned his gaze back to the fire, the flickering flames reflecting in his dark eyes, illuminating a depth of history that weighed heavily on his soul. "I had a family once. A mother and father who loved me. We lived in a small village near the mountains, far removed from the chaos of politics and battles. We were happy." The pain in his voice cut through the stillness, resonating in both Elora and Lyra's hearts.

He paused, his face tightening as the memories came crashing down. "My mother... she had the kindest heart. Always singing, always smiling. She had a way of making everything seem better, even in the darkest times. She would sing me lullabies, songs that echoed through the mountains, and her voice was like... like a warm blanket on the coldest night." His voice cracked, and for a moment, he fell silent, staring at the fire.

Elora's heart ached for him, but before she could speak, Ronan continued, his words tinged with the rawness of loss. "My father was a blacksmith. Strong, proud, and always teaching me the value of hard work and honor. He taught me how to wield a hammer and shape iron, how to build something that would last. Every evening, we'd sit together by the fire, share stories, laugh. Those nights... I thought they'd never end." His jaw clenched, his eyes distant, as if seeing something beyond the fire.

"But it ended. Just like that. The warlord's men came and took everything—burned my home, took my parents, my little sister..." His voice faltered, and the words felt like they were tearing at his chest. He swallowed hard, and when he spoke again, it was with a bitter edge. "They thought they could break me by taking the people I loved most. But they didn't break me. They made me want to burn it all down. They made me want to see the world burn with the same fire they set to my home."

Ronan paused, his gaze softening, though his jaw remained clenched. "I... I miss her. My little sister. She was... everything. She was the light of our lives. She'd follow me around, begging to come with me to the forge, to help me with whatever work I was doing, even though she was too small to carry anything. She was stubborn. She had this little laugh that was so infectious it could make even my gruff father smile. She'd run around the village, playing games with the other children, always making them laugh. And... when they came, she was there, in the middle of it all. I couldn't protect her." His voice broke for a moment, before he steadied himself.

Elora, her heart aching for him, took a breath, as though trying to absorb the pain in his words. She gently placed a hand on his arm, her voice quiet. "I'm sorry, Ronan."

Lyra, who had remained silent up until this point, spoke in a low, measured tone. "My village wasn't like that... My family wasn't mine by blood. We didn't have parents, not in the way you did. But the village—it was home. Everyone there, they cared for us like we were their own. It wasn't about being an orphan. We were all brothers and sisters." Her eyes seemed far away, as though seeing her village in her mind's eye. "I had no parents, but I had them. And now they're all gone. I've never felt so alone." She gave Ronan a sidelong glance, as if understanding the particular sting of the loss of a sibling.

The words from both Ronan and Lyra settled between them, a quiet acknowledgment of their shared grief. It wasn't just loss—they were learning, through the pain, that they had once belonged to something, and now they were fighting to reclaim something even greater.

Ronan looked at Lyra, his eyes softening, understanding dawning. "You're right. We carry it together, even if it doesn't feel that way."

Lyra gave him a slight nod, her lips pulling into a soft, sad smile. "We do." She looked toward Elora then, who seemed to be quietly processing everything. "And we're not going to let it break us."

Ronan's gaze lingered on the fire for a long moment, before he slowly returned to sharpening his blade, his movements smoother now, less frenzied. The tension between them seemed to ease, even if just a little, and for the first time in a long while, Ronan let the weight of his past settle—not as a burden, but as part of who he was.

"We fight together," he murmured, his voice firm.

Elora nodded, her voice steady as she added, "And we stand by each other."

Lyra's eyes glistened in the firelight, her heart lightened for the first time in weeks. "Together," she echoed.

"Let's get some rest," Ronan says, his voice low and steady. "We've still got a long journey ahead of us."

VIII

TALES OF THE HISTORY

The sun hung low in the sky, casting a pale, ethereal light over the ruins that stretched before them. Shadows crept across the stonework, giving the impression of a long-forgotten kingdom abandoned to the slow embrace of time. The air felt charged, thick with unspoken secrets and the whispers of long-dead magic. Elora stood at the entrance, her heart pounding in sync with the weight of the moment, a mix of anticipation and dread curling in her stomach.

"It has to be here," she whispered, a sense of destiny pulling her forward. It had taken them days—through thick forest, jagged cliffs, and ancient trails—to find this place, hidden deep in the Forgotten Forest. The villagers had spoken of it only in hushed tones, describing it as a realm forsaken by all but the oldest of magic. Now, standing at its threshold, she felt the

gravity of what lay ahead.

"This must be it," Lyra murmured, her voice low and reverent. She knelt, brushing away layers of dirt and moss to reveal intricate carvings etched into the stone floor—symbols of forgotten gods and long-dead empires. "The library of the lost sages."

Ronan stood at the edge of the clearing, his jaw clenched, scanning the perimeter with a wary eye. "We should be careful," he warned, his hand never far from the hilt of his sword. "These woods aren't known for being friendly. I don't like how quiet it is." His gaze shifted, catching movement in the shadows, and Elora felt a chill race up her spine.

Elora took a deep breath, feeling the energy pulsing faintly through the stones, like the remnants of a long-forgotten heartbeat. It called to her, a whisper in the back of her mind that tugged her forward. "We have to go in," she urged, her voice steadying with purpose. "The legend speaks of knowledge buried here... something that could help us."

Lyra glanced up, skepticism etched on her brow. "You really think these jewels are going to be the answer? They sound like a fairy tale... and not a particularly comforting one."

Elora hesitated, the truth swirling like leaves in a storm. She wasn't sure. But ever since they had uncovered the first hints of the legendary jewels, she had felt an inexplicable connection to them, as if they were part of a destiny she couldn't escape. "It's the only lead we have," she said, determination hardening her resolve. "We need every advantage we can get."

With a nod that seemed to steel her nerves, they ventured into the ruins. The moment they crossed the threshold, the air thickened, swirling around them like a living thing. The walls, lined with faded tapestries and crumbling remains of statues, hummed with energy, as if echoing the whispers of the past. Each step deeper felt like a journey through time itself.

"This place gives me the creeps," Ronan muttered, his voice low. The shadows danced in the flickering light of their torches, casting unsettling shapes along the walls. "Feels like a trap waiting to spring."

Elora nodded, but pressed forward, her heart racing. "We're close," she said, her voice barely above a whisper. Her fingers brushed against the cold stone walls, feeling the remnants of spells long since faded. They stepped into a large circular chamber, the ceiling high and domed, shadows flickering like restless spirits in the dim light.

In the center of the room, bathed in the moonlight pouring through cracks in the roof, stood an altar—old, weathered, and covered in dust. Atop it lay a single object: an ancient tome.

Lyra approached first, eyes wide with wonder. "What is this place?" Her voice trembled with excitement and apprehension.

Elora's gaze was fixated on the book, an overwhelming sense of fate washing over her. She stepped forward, her heart pounding in her chest, and gently opened the tome. Dust swirled into the air, spiraling upward before settling again. The pages were brittle, their edges yellowed with age, and the language was so ancient that it barely registered in her mind. But one word stood out, glowing faintly from the page, as if imbued with its own light: Astrion.

"The Jewels of the Stars," Elora whispered, her fingers tracing the delicate, glowing letters. "It's real."

Ronan's eyes narrowed, stepping closer, curiosity mingling with caution. "What does it say? What is this place?"

Elora scanned the page, urgency propelling her words. "The jewels," she said slowly, "are scattered across Eryndor, hidden by the sages to protect their power from those who would misuse them. Each one is tied to an element—fire, water, earth—and together, they hold the power to shape the very fabric of the world."

Lyra's voice was laced with skepticism. "And you think we can use them to stop the warlord?"

Elora looked up, her resolve hardening. "We have to. It's our only chance." But even as she spoke, doubt gnawed at her. The power these jewels held—it was immense, overwhelming. Could they truly control it? And at what cost?

Suddenly, the room trembled. The walls groaned, as though the very structure of the ruins reacted to the words they had uncovered. A low, unsettling hum filled the air, and the faint glow from the book intensified, casting eerie shadows that danced along the walls like restless spirits.

"We need to leave," Ronan said sharply, his eyes scanning the shadows as his hand moved to the hilt of his sword. With a swift motion, he drew it free, stepping in front of Elora and positioning himself between her and the threat. His instincts, honed from years of battle, screamed that they were no longer safe here. "Now."

Elora snapped the book shut, the weight of their discovery pressing down on her like a shroud. She knew that from this moment, everything had changed. The warlord was no longer their only enemy. Other forces—ancient and dangerous—were stirring.

As they fled the chamber, the wind howled through the cracks in the stone, carrying with it a chilling whisper that echoed in her mind: Power... but at what price?

IX
WARLORD.

Deep within the shadows of his fortress, the warlord gazed out at the sprawling lands of Eryndor, a cruel smile tugging at his lips. The power he had amassed over the years coursed through him like a potent elixir, intoxicating and heady. He had crushed rebellions before, silenced dissent with an iron fist, and yet something about this uprising felt different.

He turned to his lieutenant, a towering figure cloaked in dark armor. "The princess thinks she can rally the villagers against me? How quaint." His voice dripped with mockery, each word laced with disdain. "They are sheep, and she is merely a lamb among them."

His lieutenant, a loyal but brutal enforcer named Garrick, crossed his arms, watching the warlord with an expression of concern. "But she has already garnered support. The villagers are emboldened, fueled by the idea of rebellion. We cannot underestimate them."

The warlord waved a dismissive hand, his eyes narrowing. "Fear is the strongest weapon, and I shall remind them of that. A few victories will shatter their resolve, and they will fall back into submission."

He paced the dimly lit chamber, shadows dancing around him like phantoms of his past. The fortress was a testament to his conquests—a place adorned with spoils from battles long forgotten, trophies of those who had dared to oppose him. It echoed with the whispers of betrayal and bloodshed, the very essence of his rise to power. Memories flooded his mind—dark alleys where alliances were forged in blood, the fear in the eyes of those who had crossed him, the thrill of dominance that surged through his veins as he asserted his will upon the land.

"The villagers of Eryndor have always been easy prey," he mused, his voice low and contemplative. "They are too naïve to understand the depths of my ambition. They cling to their notions of honor and loyalty while I play the long game. I have given them no reason to hope, and now they dare to believe they can defy me? It is laughable."

Garrick shifted uneasily, sensing the tension that lingered in the air. "And yet, the princess's resolve is fierce. She has gathered support from the most unlikely of allies—Ronan, Lyra, and others who have suffered *under your rule. They are more than mere villagers; they are now a force that could challenge your authority."*

The warlord's lips curled into a sinister grin, a spark of amusement igniting within him. "Ah, yes. The brave little warriors who think they can change their fate. How delightful. Their defiance is but a candle in a tempest, easily extinguished." He leaned closer to Garrick, his voice a conspiratorial whisper. "But we shall not extinguish them yet. No, let them gather their forces, let them believe they have a chance. I will unleash my army upon them at the opportune moment—a demonstration of my strength that will send them scurrying back into the shadows."

His lieutenant nodded, an air of excitement building around him. "And what of the princess? She's young, but she possesses a fire that ignites those around her. We must eliminate her before she becomes a true threat."

The warlord's eyes gleamed with malice, a flicker of dark anticipation dancing across his features. "Yes, yes, of course. We'll turn their hope into despair. Send out scouts to gather intelligence on their movements. I want to know where they meet, what plans they formulate, and most importantly, where I can strike to shatter their morale."

Garrick straightened, his expression hardening. "I will see to it immediately. But may I suggest we offer them a demonstration of our might? A targeted raid on one of their gatherings could send a message—a reminder of the consequences of defiance."

The warlord stroked his chin, contemplating the idea. "A raid, you say? A clever strategy. Strike at the heart of their newly found hope. It will break their spirit and serve as a stark reminder that they are still under my thumb. We will make an example of them."

He turned away from Garrick, walking to the large map that sprawled across the table, its surface littered with markers representing villages, troop movements, and the heart of Eryndor. "Mark their strongholds. Identify their weaknesses. We will crush them swiftly and mercilessly."

Garrick leaned over the map, his finger tracing the contours of the land. "The festival they planned may provide the perfect opportunity. If we strike when they are gathered in celebration, it will be chaos. They will scatter, their resolve broken in an instant."

The warlord's laughter echoed through the chamber, a cold, merciless sound. "Yes, let us feast on their joy and turn it to ash. Prepare the men. I want my finest warriors ready to move at first light. We will show them the price of rebellion."

As Garrick moved to implement the warlord's orders, a sense of unease crept into the warlord's thoughts. There was something about Elora that unsettled him. He could not deny the flicker of fear she inspired within him, a reflection of his own insecurities. Her ability to unite the villagers sparked something deep within—a realization that power was not merely about dominance but about the hearts and minds of the people.

"Stay vigilant," he called after Garrick. "If we falter even for a moment, that flame of hope could become a wildfire. I want eyes everywhere. We cannot allow them to catch us off guard."

In the hours that followed, the warlord immersed himself in the preparations, rallying his troops, sharpening their blades, and feeding them tales of glory and conquest. Each warrior he inspired was a cog in his grand machine, a necessary piece in the game of power. He relished the anticipation, the taste of impending conflict tingling on his tongue.

As night fell, he took a moment to stand atop the fortress walls, the moon casting an ethereal glow over the landscape. He could see the distant flickers of fires in Eryndor, the sounds of laughter and music wafting through the air—a stark contrast to the grim fortress behind him.

"Let them dance in the moonlight," he muttered to himself, his voice a low growl. "Let them believe in their dreams of rebellion. When the dawn breaks, I will be there to shatter their illusions and reclaim my dominion over them."

In the dark of night, as the wind whispered through the fortress, the warlord steeled himself for the battle ahead. This was not just a war for land or power; it was a war for the very essence of his control over Eryndor. He would not allow a mere girl to stand in his way. He would crush the rebellion before it had the chance to bloom, extinguishing their hopes and dreams with the fury of a tempest.

The warlord turned from the edge of the walls, the shadows enveloping him once more as he made his way back to the heart of the fortress. Each step echoed with the promise of chaos, the thrill of impending violence electrifying the air around him.

X

A WOUNDED KINGDOM

When they returned, the village was a graveyard of ashes and broken dreams.

Elora walked through the charred ruins, her heart heavy with suffocating guilt as the echoes of destruction haunted her every step. The air was thick with the acrid scent of smoke mingling with something far worse—loss. What had once been a thriving community, vibrant and full of life, now lay in tatters, reduced to a wasteland where sorrow reigned supreme.

Children huddled together in the remnants of what had once been a schoolhouse, their wide eyes dulled to a hollow gaze, faces smudged with dirt and soot, mirroring the devastation around them. A mother wept beside the lifeless body of her child, her anguished cries tearing through the stillness, a raw sound so full of pain it felt like a dagger aimed straight for Elora's heart.

The rebellion had come too late for the village. Their numbers had swelled, but what good were armies of men and women if they could not protect the innocent?

"Elora..." Ronan's voice broke the silence, a quiet murmur laced with unspoken grief. He walked beside her, his expression dark and unreadable. The tension radiating from him was palpable, his sharp gaze scanning the ruins with a grimness that had become hauntingly familiar.

"This is what happens in war," he said tersely, his voice low and heavy with the reality of their failure. "Innocent people suffer. We've seen it time and time again. It's the cost that reverberates with every act of defiance."

Elora swallowed hard against the lump in her throat, her gaze falling to the lifeless bodies littering the ground, faces twisted in agony—echoes of lives once full of promise. "I didn't think it would be like this," she whispered, her voice trembling with the weight of grief. "I thought... I thought we could protect them. I promised them hope."

Ronan's gaze remained steady, his voice gentle yet firm as he placed a reassuring hand on her shoulder. "You can't protect everyone, Princess," he said, the softness in his eyes breaking through the armor of his demeanor. "No matter how hard you try, you cannot save them all."

Elora knelt beside a young girl, her heart breaking at the sight. She offered her a piece of bread from her satchel, an offering of compassion in a world painted with desolation. The girl looked up, wide-eyed and afraid, but there was no gratitude in her gaze, only fear cloaked in ashes. Elora's heart ached, and her resolve wavered as the enormity of it all settled over her like a suffocating storm.

"How many more villages will burn because of my rebellion?" Elora whispered, her voice a trembling thread. "How many more lives will be lost in this struggle against the warlord?"

"I promised them hope," she said, the words escaping her lips like a mournful sigh—more a prayer than a statement.

Ronan nodded, though deep sadness etched across his features mirrored her own. "You gave them something worth fighting for," he reminded her, his voice steady. "That's more than anyone else has done. They see you not just as a leader, but as someone willing to stand against the darkness. You inspire them—even now."

Elora stood, her eyes scanning the devastation around her. The warlord's forces had razed the village, their punishment swift and ruthless. "But even that may not be enough," she murmured, despair weighing heavily in her chest. "We'll never rebuild what's been lost; their unheard screams echo in my mind."

"But we can ensure their deaths mean something," Ronan said, a fire igniting within him as he looked at her, determination pushing against the despair like a lighthouse in the storm. "Every drop of blood shed for freedom will reverberate. We must use that to fuel our fight, to ignite the flames of rebellion."

Elora's breath hitched, a newfound determination flickering inside her. "I won't let this happen again," she vowed, her voice trembling with raw emotion—the promise of a warrior who had witnessed too many tragedies. "I swear it."

Ronan nodded, his expression grim, though a flicker of resolve ignited in his eyes. "We'll make them pay for what they've done, Elora. But we'll do it on our terms, with our honor intact. We'll turn this pain into our strength, and we'll rise again, together."

A shadow fell over them, and Lyra's quiet voice broke through the weight of the moment. "It's not just about vengeance. It's about giving them something they didn't have—something the warlord and his men can never take away."

They turned to find Lyra standing a few paces away, her posture stiff but determined. She had been walking in silence, her eyes taking in the same horrors, but her heart was heavier still. She had known the grief of losing a village, a home, but this—this felt different. This was the death of everything she had ever fought for. Her childhood, her innocence, had been shattered long ago, but these children? These survivors—they would need more than vengeance. They would need a future.

Lyra's eyes lingered on the children huddled in the ruins of the schoolhouse, their faces etched with fear, their innocence lost in the fire. She walked over to them, her steps slow, as if she could feel the weight of the village's memory pressing down on her.

Elora, watching her, followed quietly. The weight of their shared grief hung thick in the air, but Lyra didn't look back. She didn't need to. The children stared at her as if she were a ghost, but in their gazes, there was also a flicker of recognition—a faint spark of hope.

"They don't need to be afraid anymore," Lyra said softly, kneeling down in front of the group. "I know what it's like to lose everything. To lose your family, your home." She paused, her voice faltering slightly, but she steadied herself. "But you're not alone. You'll never be alone again."

The children hesitated, but Lyra reached into her satchel and pulled out a few pieces of dried fruit. She offered them silently, her eyes softening with an understanding that only someone who had survived such loss could offer. Slowly, a young boy reached out, taking a piece from her hand, his fingers trembling. And with that small gesture, something inside Lyra cracked open, and she allowed herself to feel a flicker of hope.

Elora watched her, feeling the weight of the moment. Lyra had always been strong, but in this moment, she was something more—a beacon of quiet strength that spoke not of vengeance, but of solidarity.

Turning back to Ronan, Elora gave a slow, deliberate nod. "We will rebuild. Not just the village, but the heart of our rebellion. We'll protect them. We'll protect everyone."

Ronan's gaze softened, his voice low but steady. "Yes. We rise from the ashes of this kingdom and build something better, something that cannot be taken.

Together."

The air around them shifted, and a resolve greater than any single person burned between them. Their grief, though heavy, became a source of power—not in the destruction of their enemies, but in the creation of something worth fighting for.

With one last glance at the village, Elora stood tall, her heart no longer broken but forged anew. "This war will not define us," she declared. "We will. We will choose who we become."

Lyra looked at the children one last time, a quiet smile crossing her face. "And they will grow stronger because of it."

XI

BETRAYAL IN THE RANKS

The campfire crackled weakly, casting long, dancing shadows across the group huddled amidst the forest. The air, once filled with camaraderie and laughter, was now thick with tension—each word spoken laced with suspicion, every glance punctured with mistrust. The rebellion, once a united force, was fracturing, and the fractures felt like daggers embedding deep into Elora's resolve.

Seated in the circle were memories of laughter and celebration, but they had all but diminished in the face of mounting unease. Over the past few weeks, something had felt amiss—whispers echoing through the trees, furtive glances exchanged in moments of hesitation, and shadows lurking in corners where trust had once flourished. The cracks in their alliance were growing wider, the trust they had built beginning to slip through their fingers like sand.

The flickering firelight illuminated the faces of the rebels, each one wearing a mask of uncertainty. Joren, a newer recruit who had joined their endeavor just a few weeks prior, sat in silence, his wiry frame consumed by anxiety. Elora had welcomed him into their ranks, believing his presence would strengthen their cause. But now, as Ronan's suspicions hung heavy in the air, Elora couldn't shake the feeling that their decision had been a grave mistake.

"I think we have a traitor in our midst," Ronan declared bluntly, his voice slicing through the thick silence like a blade. His dark eyes scanned the group, pinpointing their unease, his hand resting on the hilt of his sword, a specter of authority dressed in doubts, ready to bare the weight of his suspicions. The words hung like a noose, tightening around their throats.

Elora's heart raced at the accusation, the weight of it pressing down on her chest. "Ronan, are you certain?" she asked, her voice barely above a whisper, yet trembling with concern. The thought of betrayal within their ranks was a bitter pill to swallow.

Lyra looked up sharply from her place by the fire, feigning both surprise and confusion. "What are you talking about?" she queried, bewilderment etched on her face, yet there was an undercurrent of fear lurking below the surface of her words.

Ronan shot to his feet, his rage palpable in every tense muscle. "Follow me," his voice barely controlled. Without waiting for a response, he stormed ahead, his steps hard and purposeful. His fury was undeniable, burning in his every movement. It was clear that wherever he was leading them, it was somewhere Joren would feel the weight of his wrath.

Ronan strode up to Joren, his presence looming like a storm about to break. Joren stood abruptly, shifting uncomfortably, his forced innocence faltering under Ronan's cold gaze. "I've seen you sneaking off at night," Ronan's voice was low, each word cutting through the silence. "Disappearing into the woods. What's been going on?" He leaned in slightly, his challenge unmistakable, and the tension in the group thickened, waiting for Joren's response.

Joren's demeanor shifted, his earlier bravado crumbling under the weight of Ronan's glare. "I…I wasn't sneaking. I was just scouting, checking for threats, making sure we weren't being followed!" His words spilled forth, laden with desperation as he attempted to ward off the growing accusation.

"Scouting?" Ronan's eyes narrowed, his suspicion so thick it seemed to hang in the air like smoke. "Or perhaps you've been reporting back to the warlord?" His voice hardened, each word a hammer strike. "Your movements have been far too... convenient. Our camps hit with pinpoint precision—like someone knew exactly where to strike. You expect us to believe that's just coincidence?" The disdain in his tone was palpable, and Elora could feel the air grow heavy with tension, the fragile thread holding the group together threatening to snap at any moment.

A heavy silence descended upon the group, thick and oppressive, as if the very air had turned to stone. The tension crackled, electric and suffocating, tightening around their chests. Each person felt it, the weight of the moment pressing in on them, but it was Elora whose heart pounded hardest, her thoughts racing with unsettling doubt. Could it be true? Was it possible that Joren, who had always seemed so earnest, could be betraying them from within? The thought gnawed at her, more disturbing than any enemy they'd faced before.

"Stop!" Elora's voice rang out, cutting through the tension like a whip. She sprang to her feet, positioning herself between Ronan and Joren, her body trembling with urgency. Her chest heaved with each rapid breath as she faced Ronan, her eyes fierce. "We don't know anything for certain," she continued, her tone unwavering. "We can't just throw accusations around without proof." The words hung in the air, a fragile plea for reason in the midst of chaos.

Yet, even as she spoke, doubt began to fester in the corners of her mind, gnawing at her like a silent predator. The warlord's forces had grown unnervingly precise in their strikes, their ambushes too well-coordinated to be dismissed as mere coincidence. Each passing day, the shadows of suspicion deepened, creeping further into her thoughts. Elora couldn't help but wonder—how far had the betrayal truly spread? How many among them had already turned? The question echoed in her mind, unspoken yet impossibly heavy.

Before Joren could finish, Ronan moved like a storm, his hand shooting out to grab him. "You won't speak up like this," he snarled, his voice low and threatening.

But as he reached for Joren, Elora stepped between them, blocking his path. Ronan paused, his breath sharp and controlled. For a long moment, he just stared at her, his gaze flickering with something unreadable. Then, without a word, he took a step back, his jaw tightening, and turned away. The tension lingered in the air, but for now, the confrontation was over.

"We need proof before we act." Elora's voice was steady, though her heart pounded in her chest. As the weight of her own words settled, she realized just how delicate their next steps would be. If they followed this course, they'd be walking a fine line—between justice and vengeance, with everything hanging on the choice they made.

Ronan's jaw clenched, the anger still smoldering in his eyes, but he nodded, the tension in his shoulders easing—just barely—as he gave in to her words. "Then we'll watch him," he said, his voice low and dangerous. "And if he slips up, I'll deal with it. No mercy, no hesitation." His tone was final, a silent vow wrapped in threat, but the edge softened just enough under her gaze..

Joren sat back down, his face drained of color, but Elora saw the fear etched into his features. She didn't know whether it was the fear of an innocent man at the mercy of unjust accusations or the guilt of a traitor who already understood his time was short. Either way, the bond of trust among them had been irrevocably fractured, cracked like glass in a violent storm.

As the fire crackled and the night enveloped them in its dark embrace, Elora felt the weight of uncertainty tightening around her like chains. The trust they had painstakingly nurtured was fraying, replaced with simmering anxiety and the unsettling fear of betrayal lurking in the shadows.

No longer would the rebels be able to move as one; instead, they found themselves embattled in suspicion, and the specter of distrust loomed ominously over the rebellion. The warlord was not the only enemy they faced now; doubt itself had settled within their ranks, threatening to consume them from the inside out.

The night wore on, each minute stretching into an eternity, as Elora wrestled with her thoughts. She glanced at Ronan, who sat apart from the group, his jaw set in determination, but the tension radiating from him was like a living entity, palpable and unsettling. Lyra remained by her side, the silence between them heavy with unspoken words.

"What do we do now?" Lyra finally asked, breaking the silence, her voice barely above a whisper.

Elora took a deep breath, steeling herself. "We watch, we wait, and we prepare. But we must also remember what we're fighting for." Her resolve strengthened, knowing that unity was their greatest weapon against the encroaching darkness. "We cannot let fear dictate our actions."

Lyra nodded, though uncertainty still clouded her features. "Just be careful, Elora. This suspicion... it can tear us apart if we're not vigilant."

As the flames flickered and danced in the night, Elora felt the weight of her role as a leader press down upon her. She would not allow betrayal to become their downfall. She would protect her comrades, rally their spirits, and steer them through the storm of doubt. With renewed determination, she resolved to uncover the truth and restore the bonds that had begun to splinter.

XII

SHATTERED BONDS

The air in the camp hung heavy with palpable tension, each breath laden with the weight of suspicion that had settled like a storm cloud over the rebellion. The once-vibrant camaraderie had dimmed, replaced by unspoken dread and uneasy glances that had become the common currency of their interactions. The accusations against Joren had cast a long shadow, fracturing the fragile alliances and eroding the trust they had built together like a sandcastle threatened by the tide.

Elora stood at the edge of the camp, her heart aching as she surveyed the faces of her companions. Once filled with laughter and warmth, now twisted with doubt, each face told a story of turmoil. Ronan had grown colder, more distant—his eyes perpetually locked in a state of vigilance, like a hawk poised to descend on its prey. He no longer approached her with the casual familiarity she had cherished; instead, he hovered at the fringes, his protective instincts morphing into an emotional barrier.

Lyra, usually so vibrant and quick to smile, had become withdrawn, her sharp gaze continually scanning the perimeter of their camp for threats—both from within and without. Each passing day, the laughter that had once echoed around their fire evaporated, leaving behind an unshakeable feeling of distrust, like a rancid odor polluting the air.

"Are you alright?" Lyra's voice broke through Elora's thoughts, soft and tinged with concern. She approached cautiously, her eyes searching Elora's face for fragments of the spirited leader she had once known.

Elora turned to face her, forcing a smile that faltered under the pressure of grief and uncertainty. "No," she admitted, the vulnerability of her admission weaving through the fabric of her being. "I'm not."

Lyra sighed, crossing her arms over her chest, her body language betraying her distress. "This whole situation... it's tearing us apart. Joren, the accusations, the constant fear... suspicion—it's too much to bear."

Elora nodded, sadness enveloping her like a shroud. "I know," she whispered, her heart heavy with the knowledge that the rebellion was being crushed from within. "But what choice do we have? We can't stop now—not when the warlord's forces are closing in. He won't wait for us to heal."

Lyra's expression remained somber, yet a fierce determination burned beneath the surface. "I just don't want to lose you, Elora. Or Ronan. Or anyone else."

"You won't," Elora declared, though the words felt hollow, echoing in the iron depths of doubt. She knew the flicker of resolve in her heart was fragile, just like their bonds. The truth was that something vital—the sense of safety and trust—had already been torn asunder. They had lost pieces of themselves during this journey, and she wasn't certain if they could reclaim what had been shattered, particularly at this perilous moment.

As Lyra stepped back from her side, turning her gaze toward the modest fire that crackled and spat sparks into the dark sky, Elora's heart ached with a profound sense of loss. She was haunted by the shadows lurking beyond the campfire glow, shadows filled with questions and fears: How could she lead them through this storm of suspicion? Had Joren truly betrayed them, or were they condemning an innocent soul?

With a heavy heart, Elora turned her gaze back to the camp. She could feel the fractures deepening, the bonds they had painstakingly woven threatening to fray completely. But beneath the turbulence stirring within her chest, a small ember flickered with *resilience—an echo of hope that refused to be snuffed out.*

She would not let this rebellion fail. She would not let the warlord win. They had come too far, sacrificed too much to let everything unravel now. Elora took a deep breath, steeling herself for the tumultuous road ahead. The bonds between them might be cracked and splintered, but she would work tirelessly to mend them, to support the fragile threads threatening to snap.

As the moon rose high in the night sky, its silvery light bathed the camp in an ethereal glow, a stark contrast to the darkness creeping into their hearts. Elora found herself wandering away from the camp, drawn by an overwhelming need for solitude. She needed to think, to gather her thoughts without the weight of her companions' suspicions pressing down on her.

The forest around her was alive with the sounds of the night—crickets chirping, the rustle of leaves in the gentle breeze—but the beauty of it all felt distant, like a fading memory. She found a clearing bathed in moonlight, a sanctuary where she could breathe freely without the suffocating tension of the camp.

As she stood there, her thoughts drifted to the beginning of their rebellion, to the hope that had ignited within them when they had first banded together against the warlord. They had been fueled by a shared desire for freedom, a collective dream of reclaiming their homeland. But now, that dream felt fragile, the bonds of unity fraying at the edges.

"What have I done?" she whispered to herself, the words tumbling out in despair. "Have I led them into a trap? Have I sacrificed their trust for my own ambition?"

Elora sank to her knees, her heart heavy with the weight of her responsibilities. It was in this moment of vulnerability that she heard a rustle behind her. Instinctively, she reached for her dagger, her senses heightened as she turned to face the sound.

"Easy, Princess," came a familiar voice from the shadows. It was Ronan, stepping into the moonlight, his expression inscrutable. "I didn't mean to startle you."

"What are you doing here?" Elora asked, her voice steadying as she tucked the dagger away. "You should be with the others."

"I needed to clear my head too," he admitted, moving closer. The tension between them was palpable, a tightrope stretched thin. "This whole situation... it's been eating away at me."

Elora studied him, seeing the conflict etched into his features. "What are we going to do, Ronan? I can feel the fractures deepening. If we don't address this soon, we'll lose everything we've fought for."

Ronan sighed, running a hand through his dark hair. "I've been thinking about that. We need to confront Joren directly, but with caution. If he is innocent, we need to find a way to reassure him. If he's not... then we need to be prepared."

Elora nodded, understanding the weight of his words. "But how do we approach this without further damaging the trust within our ranks?"

Ronan stepped closer, the moonlight casting a soft glow on his features. "We'll do it together. We can't let fear dictate our actions. We must show our people that we're united, that we can withstand this storm."

As she looked into his eyes, Elora felt a flicker of hope ignite within her. "You're right. We'll confront Joren, but we'll do it as a team. We need to remind everyone why we're fighting, why we started this rebellion in the first place."

Ronan's expression softened, a warmth returning to his gaze. "And we'll find a way to mend these shattered bonds. We have to believe that our unity is stronger than the forces trying to tear us apart."

With a renewed sense of purpose, Elora took a deep breath, the tension in her chest easing as she stood beside Ronan. "Together," she affirmed, the word solidifying their resolve.

As they made their way back to the camp, Elora felt a sense of clarity wash over her.

XIII

A SNAKE AMONG THE GRASS

The dawn broke over the horizon, casting pale golden light across the remnants of the rebellion's camp. Elora stood at the edge of the forest, her silhouette framed by the rising sun, a fleeting reminder that even in the darkest of times, light could pierce through. Yet, as beautiful as the dawn was, it felt like a betrayal, a mocking contrast to the turmoil brewing within her.

The camp had settled into a restless silence, a far cry from the laughter and energy that once filled the air. Each member of their band was lost in their own thoughts, weighed down by the burdens of doubt and fear. Elora's heart ached at the sight; she felt responsible for the fractures that had formed, the seeds of mistrust that had sprouted in their midst.

Ronan approached her, his presence both comforting and heavy. The shadows that clung to him seemed darker than before, as if the night had marked him in a way he couldn't shake. "We need to make a decision," he said, his voice low but firm. "Staying here is a risk. The warlord's forces are regrouping, and I fear it won't be long before they come for us."

Elora turned to face him, searching his face for answers she didn't have. "I know. But what if Joren is innocent? If we move against him now…" She trailed off, the thought alone twisting her stomach into knots. She couldn't bear the idea of condemning someone who might not be guilty.

Ronan's eyes hardened. "And what if he isn't? We can't afford to take that risk. If he's a traitor, he could lead the warlord straight to us." His frustration bubbled just beneath the surface, a tension she could feel echoing in the space between them.

"I'm not saying we should ignore the threat. I just think we need to gather more information before we act," Elora replied, clenching her fists at her sides. The last thing she wanted was for the rebellion to devolve into an internal conflict, where suspicion turned comrades into enemies.

Lyra emerged from the shadows of the trees, her expression a mix of concern and resolve. "We could observe Joren without him knowing. If he's planning to betray us, we'll catch him in the act." Her voice held a flicker of hope, a strategy that could preserve their fragile unity while also keeping them safe.

Elora felt a surge of gratitude toward Lyra for suggesting a way to navigate the tightrope of their situation. "That could work. But we'll need to be cautious. If he senses we're watching, he might change his behavior or even flee."

Ronan crossed his arms, a frown marring his features. "It's dangerous. But it might be our best option. If Joren is truly working for the warlord, we need to find out before he puts us all at risk."

"Then it's settled," Elora declared, a new determination settling in her heart. "We'll keep a close eye on him. But we do this carefully—no accusations until we have proof."

The moonlight barely touched the edges of the forest, leaving the clearing in a dark, cold embrace. Joren stood there, his posture tense as he spoke to the shadowy figure who had emerged from the trees. Elora and Ronan crouched in the underbrush, their breaths shallow, barely daring to move.

She could hear his words clearly now—his voice laced with a mixture of bitterness and quiet resolve.

"It's almost time," Joren said, his voice steady, betraying none of the inner turmoil that Elora had come to expect. "Once the princess is out of the picture, I'll have control. I'll have the power the rebels need. All she does is lead them with that crown of hers—she's a symbol, nothing more. The warlord—he sees that. He's offering me a position. His right hand." His lips curled into a faint, smug smile. "I'll make the decision for them. He knows how to win this war."

The figure before him was cloaked, their features hidden in the shadows, but their voice was cold, calculating. "So, you're sure this will work? You'll be in control."

Joren's eyes flicked to the ground before meeting the figure's hidden gaze. "She doesn't deserve this—I do. She was born into power. I've had to earn every scrap of it. The warlord's already offered me a place by his side. Think of it—a position of real influence. I won't have to hide anymore. No more pretending. The rebels will follow me, or they'll fall." His eyes glinted with ambition, his next words bitter. "And that princess... she's nothing but an obstacle."

Elora's stomach twisted with disgust as she heard the venom in his voice. She had known Joren's loyalty was always in question, but this... this was betrayal in its purest form. He wasn't just betraying them—he was seeking power at their expense.

Ronan tensed beside her, his muscles coiling with barely contained rage. But she held her ground, motioning for him to wait. She needed to hear more.

Joren leaned in, his tone dropping as if sharing some private confidence. "I'll keep her distracted. Alone. The warlord needs her gone for good if he's to reclaim what's rightfully his. When the time comes, I'll make sure she doesn't see it coming. Then I'll be the one leading this rebellion—and maybe more."

Elora's heart sank as the final pieces of the puzzle clicked into place. Not only was Joren a traitor, but he had already chosen his side. He wasn't in this for the cause; he was in it for power, for the promise of a throne.

The cloak of uncertainty fell from her shoulders, replaced by a cold clarity. It was over. Joren had made his choice.

Without warning, Ronan surged forward, his presence a force of nature that seemed to freeze the night air around them. His movements were precise, deliberate—not a shout, but an intense, simmering power that radiated from him like the edge of a blade. He didn't need words to make his fury known.

Joren's eyes widened as he turned, too slow to react. The sight of Ronan coming toward him with his sword drawn was enough to freeze him in place, his mouth opening in a reflexive plea.

"No," Joren said, stumbling back, hands raised in a futile gesture. "Ronan, please! You don't understand—I had to do this! You don't know what they've promised me."

Ronan didn't speak, his expression unreadable, but his sword was unwavering. He took another step, forcing Joren to retreat until his back hit a tree, the panic in his eyes growing.

But then the figure—hidden in the cloak—made a sudden movement, slipping into the darkness without a sound. One second they were there, and the next, they were gone. Vanished. Not even a whisper remained in the space they had occupied.

Ronan's eyes snapped to the shadows, his body tensing like a predator scenting prey, but the figure had already escaped into the night.

"Damn it," he muttered, his voice low and dangerous, though his focus remained on Joren. The sudden disappearance of the figure didn't faze him. Joren was still the immediate threat.

Elora stepped forward, closing the distance between herself and the traitor. "So, this is how it ends?" she asked, her voice deceptively calm. "You sold us out, Joren. All for a taste of power."

Joren's face twisted with frustration, his fists clenching at his sides. "I wasn't betraying you! I was trying to save what I could! You don't understand! The warlord offered me a chance—real power. He offered me a future that doesn't end in some rebel camp with no chance of ever winning. You think you're the only one who's sacrificed, Elora? You think I didn't have a choice?"

Elora stepped closer, her gaze unflinching. "You had a choice," she said, each word sharp and deliberate. "But you chose to stab us in the back. You chose to betray your comrades, to betray me. And for what? A promise from the warlord? You never understood what we were fighting for."

Joren's eyes flashed with anger, but it was tinged with fear now. "I understand more than you think," he spat. "I understand that this war was never about freedom—it's about survival. The warlord is real power. He wins. You and your noble ideals... they won't keep us alive."

Ronan's voice was low, but the threat in it was clear. "You've put us all in danger. You think the warlord will keep his word when he's done using you?" His eyes narrowed, the weight of his anger contained but palpable. "You think you can betray us and walk away?"

Joren swallowed hard, his face drawn in a mixture of shame and stubborn defiance. "I had no choice..."

"You always have a choice," Ronan replied coldly, stepping closer, his presence suffocating. "But you chose wrong."

Lyra appeared then, stepping from the shadows with her usual measured grace. She regarded Joren silently for a moment, her eyes flicking to Elora and Ronan. Finally, she spoke, her voice calm, but firm. "We've heard enough. We'll deal with him later. But we can't waste any more time on him now. The warlord is still out there—and this?" She nodded toward Joren, still cowering against the tree. "This is a distraction we can't afford."

Elora gave her a brief nod, then turned her gaze back to Joren. "You'll stay alive for now. But don't mistake our mercy for weakness. If you so much as breathe a word of betrayal again, I'll have no choice but to end it."

Joren's eyes flicked from Ronan's sword to Elora's steely gaze, and for a brief moment, he seemed to shrink under the weight of their fury. But he remained silent, *his face a mask of helplessness and bitterness.*

Ronan turned, his sword still drawn but lowered, his body coiled in restrained tension. He wasn't done with Joren, not by a long shot. He met Elora's eyes briefly, the intensity of his stare lingering longer than necessary. There was something unspoken between them, but it was fleeting, just a shadow of connection that neither of them fully understood.

Elora gave one last look at Joren, her decision made, and then she turned toward the path leading back to the village. "Let's go," she said quietly, her tone resolute. "We need to get back. The warlord isn't waiting."

Ronan nodded curtly. "You go ahead, princess. I'll follow."

Elora didn't hear the sharpness in Ronan's voice as she moved ahead. She was focused on the mission now, the burden of her decision pressing down on her shoulders. But Ronan's mind was elsewhere. As soon as Elora had turned her back, he stepped in closer to Joren—his movements silent and deliberate, a predator closing in on prey.

Joren, sensing the shift, looked up at Ronan, his face pale. His hands were shaking. He wanted to say something—plead for mercy—but the words wouldn't come.

Ronan's voice was low, cutting through the silence between them. "You think you've won?" he asked softly, dangerously. "You think you're walking away from this? You're not. Not after what you've done."

Joren opened his mouth to speak, but Ronan's glare silenced him.

"You've made your choice, traitor," Ronan said, his words growing colder. "And now, you'll live with the consequences. The princess may have spared you, but I haven't. You're a threat to us, and I won't let that slide."

Ronan's hand tightened around the hilt of his sword, though he didn't raise it. The threat was in his voice, in the icy calm of his tone.

"Cross us again," Ronan whispered, just loud enough for Joren to hear, "and I'll make sure you don't live long enough to regret it. You'll be dead before the sun rises."

Joren's breath caught in his throat. He wanted to protest, to beg for his life, but all he could do was nod, his mind racing with panic.

"Remember this, Joren," Ronan said, his voice low, almost cold with conviction. "There are worse things than death. Betray the princess again, and you'll wish for death."

Ronan's hand never left the hilt of his sword as he stepped back, his gaze lingering on Joren for one last moment. The traitor sat there, his shoulders slumped, a mixture of bitterness and fear playing across his face. But Ronan was done talking. Words had failed, and now only actions would speak.

With a sharp motion, Ronan grabbed Joren by the arm, his grip like iron, forcing him to his feet. Joren stumbled, caught off guard by the sudden brutality, but Ronan didn't let him go. He hauled him upright with a sneer, his face cold and unreadable.

"Move," Ronan muttered, his voice low and laced with a sharp edge.

Joren tried to shake him off, his voice a strained whisper. "Let me go."

But Ronan didn't respond. Instead, he yanked Joren forward, pulling him along with an almost casual cruelty. Joren's steps were slow, hesitant, as he was *dragged behind Ronan like a puppet on a string. Each tug on his arm made it clear that Ronan wasn't just guiding him; he was forcing him, dragging him toward the village with a silent, smoldering fury that radiated from him like the heat of a furnace.*

Elora and Lyra were already several paces ahead, their backs turned, but neither of them looked back. Elora had made her decision, and Lyra—always the pragmatic one—seemed content to let Ronan deal with the traitor in whatever way he saw fit.

Ronan didn't care if they were watching. His focus was entirely on Joren. With every step, he tightened his grip, dragging the traitor forward like a prisoner, a grim reminder that Joren's fate had been sealed the moment he chose the warlord's side.

Joren's breath hitched with each step, his face contorting with a mix of frustration and humiliation. He wanted to fight back, to scream, to demand his release, but the weight of Ronan's cold determination held him in place.

By the time they caught up to Elora and Lyra, Ronan's grip on Joren's arm had tightened to the point where the traitor could barely keep up. He was breathing heavily, his eyes flicking between Ronan and the distant figures of Elora and Lyra.

Ronan didn't even look at Elora as he finally released Joren, shoving him forward with a swift, calculated movement. Joren stumbled, catching himself before he could fall, but the message was clear—he had no choice but to follow, no choice but to live with the consequences of his betrayal.

"Don't get comfortable," Ronan muttered, his voice low enough that only Joren could hear. "You're still a liability. And if you think you're walking out of this without consequences, you're wrong."

Joren didn't respond, his mouth a thin, tight line. His shoulders were hunched, his face a mask of bitterness.

As they walked toward the village, the distance between them and the rebellion grew. But for Joren, the real distance had already been set: the line between life and death, between loyalty and treason, was now a chasm that would never be crossed again.

The warlord was still out there. The rebellion was fractured, but the fight wasn't over yet. Not by a long shot.

XIV

BENEATH THE WEIGHT OF BETRAYAL

The air was thick with unspoken tension as the rebels gathered around the flickering fire, shadows dancing across their weary faces. The revelation of Joren's betrayal still hung in the air like a storm cloud, suffocating any hope of peace. Elora stood at the edge of the camp, her hands clasped tightly in front of her, the weight of their collective gaze pressing down on her. She could feel the fracture in the group, the crack in their unity—brought on by one man's choices.

Joren stood near the fire, his shoulders hunched in shame, the fear in his eyes an open wound. His once-steady presence had been reduced to something fragile, untrustworthy. The camp had fallen into an uneasy silence, each rebel lost in their own thoughts, unsure whether to cast their lot with him or cast him out.

Ronan broke the silence first, his voice low but brimming with fury. He paced in front of Joren, each step deliberate, controlled—like a predator circling its prey. "You risked everything by telling the warlord about us, Joren. You put us all in danger," he spat, his jaw clenched, the muscles in his neck taut with anger. "How do you explain that? How do you explain the fact that you sold us out for a handful of promises?"

Joren's gaze dropped to the ground, his fists trembling at his sides, the weight of his choices pressing on him. "I—I didn't think it through," he muttered, voice tight with regret and fear. "The warlord... he promised me a place beside him. Power, control... I was blinded by it. And then I saw what he could do—what he does to villages, to people like us... I didn't know what to believe anymore. I thought... I thought it was the only way to survive."

Elora could feel the desperation in his voice, but it was drowned by the weight of his betrayal. Her gaze shifted to the others, each of them looking at Joren with a mixture of doubt and disbelief.

Lyra spoke next, her voice colder than Elora had ever heard it. "You thought you could protect us? By selling us out to the warlord? How can we ever trust you again, after that? How do we know you won't do it again when the next promise comes along?"

Elora's heart clenched at the venom in Lyra's words. This was a moment that could tear them apart if they let it. Her hand tightened into a fist as she stepped forward, hoping her words would offer some thread of unity. "We need to understand that fear can drive people to do terrible things," she said, her voice calm but laced with an unshakable sorrow. "Joren's actions were a betrayal, but we have to acknowledge the fear that pushed him to it. Fear for his family, fear for his own life. None of us are immune to that. It's what makes us human."

Ronan's eyes narrowed, disbelief flashing across his face. "So you're saying we just forgive him because he was scared? We can't afford to be that weak, Elora. We're at war. And we can't have someone like him—someone who's already betrayed us—walking among us."

Elora's chest tightened, the weight of leadership settling heavily on her shoulders. She understood Ronan's anger—it mirrored her own. But if they let fear guide them now, they would lose everything. "No, Ronan. I'm not saying we forget what he did. But we can't let our anger tear us apart. If we do that, we're no better than the warlord. We need to move forward, even if it means accepting Joren's help—on our terms."

Joren's eyes flickered with something like hope. "I can help. I know their movements. I know their plans. I know where they're vulnerable. If you'll let me, I can still help you take them down." His voice cracked with a mix of regret and pleading.

Ronan stepped closer, his hands still clenched, but his voice was controlled now—each word measured. "You want to help us? Then prove it. If you betray us again....you remember very well."

Elora met Ronan's gaze, her heart pounding in her chest. She knew the danger of giving Joren another chance. But she also knew that without his information, they might as well be walking blind into the warlord's army. "We'll watch him. But for now, he stays. If we don't let him help, we risk our lives. We can't afford that."

Joren's face was a mixture of gratitude and guilt. "I won't let you down. I'll do whatever it takes to make it right."

Lyra, standing at the edge of the group, exhaled sharply, her tone quiet but filled with sorrow. "You say that now. But actions speak louder than words, Joren. I just... I don't want anyone else to die because of you."

Elora's heart ached for her, but there was no time for hesitation. "We don't have the luxury of waiting for perfection," she said, her voice hardening with resolve. "We have to keep moving forward."

The group fell into a heavy silence, the fire crackling and popping in the stillness. It was a silence filled with doubt, with hesitation. They were a family torn apart by betrayal, and though they might stitch themselves back together, they would never be the same.

That night, long after the others had gone to sleep, Elora sat alone by the fire. The warmth of the embers was a hollow comfort. Her mind drifted back to the ancient tales of Eryndor—of the legendary jewels that could turn the tide of war, said to be hidden in the forgotten corners of the land. If those jewels were real, if they could be found, they could give the rebellion a fighting chance.

But was it worth the risk? Was it worth trusting someone who had already shown himself willing to betray them?

As dawn broke, Elora called the rebels together. The air felt heavier this morning, thick with the weight of their collective uncertainty.

"We can't afford to be stuck in this place of indecision," she said, her voice clear and resolute, though the doubt lingered in her chest. "Joren has agreed to help us, and we'll use that to our advantage. But we need to focus on the bigger picture. The warlord's forces are regrouping, and if we don't act soon, we'll be too late."

Ronan's eyes were still sharp, his skepticism lingering. "What do you have in mind?"

"We need to find the legendary jewels," Elora said, the words leaving her lips with a force that surprised even her. "I know it sounds like a gamble. But if they exist, they could be the key to our survival."

Lyra furrowed her brow, her voice cautious. "You really believe they exist?"

Elora nodded. "I have to. We've fought for so long with nothing but hope and scraps. If we continue this way—without strength, without the means to actually defeat the warlord—we'll fall. One by one."

Joren, standing at the back of the group, hesitated, then stepped forward. "I've heard rumors. Whispers about where the jewels might be hidden. If we move quickly, we might be able to find them before the warlord even knows we're after them."

Ronan's skepticism and hatred was still clear, but he nodded slowly. "It's a risk. But it might be our best chance."

Elora felt a flicker of hope stir within her. "Then it's settled. We'll search for the jewels. And when we find them, we'll take the warlord down."

The group rallied around her, their resolve firming with the shared mission. They were no longer just a scattered rebellion. They were a force with purpose. And though the path ahead was uncertain, they would walk it together—bound by the fragile hope that they might yet reclaim everything they had lost.

XV
JEWELS OF ERYNDOR

Elora knew that they needed more than mere tactics and courage to secure a lasting change in Eryndor. The key to their salvation lay in an ancient legend—the story of three powerful jewels, each imbued with extraordinary power.

As the shadows flickered, Elora unfurled a tattered map she had discovered among the village's relics. The parchment was old and weathered, the ink faded but still legible. "These jewels," she began, her voice steady but urgent, "They are said to represent the core elements of our land: fire, water, and earth. They were forged by the ancient guardians of Eryndor, and if we can find them, we can wield their power against the warlord."

Ronan, his brow furrowed in thought, leaned closer, his curiosity piqued. "I've heard whispers of these jewels, but I always dismissed them as folklore. How do we know they even exist?"

"Legends often hold more truth than we realize," Elora replied, determination hardening her voice. "The stories have survived for centuries for a reason. They echo through our history, and if we can locate them and harness their power, we might finally have a chance to shift the balance in our favor."

Elora glanced at the map, tracing her finger over the markings with care. "The legends mention three specific locations: the Cave of Flames, the Temple of Tides, and the Grove of Stone. Each jewel is said to be protected by ancient magic, and only those deemed worthy can claim them."

Lyra's eyes flashed with recognition as a thought struck her. "Wait... I remember something," she said, her voice rising with the clarity of a long-forgotten memory. "An old woman from my village once told me about the Jewels... and their powers. She used to speak of them when I was a child."

She paused, collecting her thoughts as the memories returned. "There's Emberheart, the Jewel from the Caves of Fire. When wielded, it grants the bearer the power to summon torrents of searing flames, turning enemies to ash with a single wave. Fire can be shaped into walls for defense, or hurled as blazing projectiles to incinerate anything in its path. But that's not all—Emberheart also amplifies the user's strength and speed, making them a whirlwind of destruction in battle. It turns its wielder into a force of nature, hard to match on the battlefield."

Lyra took a breath, moving to the next Jewel. "Then there's the Abyssal Tear, from the Temple of Tides. It allows the bearer to control water in all its forms—summoning crashing waves, conjuring whirlpools to trap enemies, or even creating calm waters for healing. In times of dire need, it can call upon the depths themselves, unleashing a tidal wave to obliterate foes or clear obstacles. The Abyssal Tear also grants the ability to breathe underwater and enhanced swimming skills, allowing its user to move freely through aquatic environments. It's as much a tool for survival as it is for battle."

Lyra hesitated before continuing, her voice softening as she spoke of the last Jewel. "And then there's Verdant's Heart, the Jewel from the Grove of Stone. This one gives the bearer dominion over nature itself. With it, they can cause plants to grow at will—summoning thick vines to entangle enemies, creating barriers of thorny briars, or even healing wounds by accelerating the growth of medicinal plants. In combat, Verdant's Heart can summon the earth itself, erupting with foliage to shield allies or hide them in a thick underbrush. It also strengthens the user's body, making them more resilient and able to recover quickly from injuries. The bearer of Verdant's Heart is attuned to the rhythms of the natural world, sensing even the slightest disturbance in the wilderness."

Lyra fell silent for a moment, as though the weight of the Jewels' powers settled over her.

Elora, who had been listening intently, nodded slowly, processing the flood of information. "Right..." she said quietly, her tone heavy with the implications of what Lyra had just shared. "So the Jewels are more than just powerful—they could change everything..."

Ronan crossed his arms, skepticism dancing in his eyes. "So, we just stroll in, ask for the jewels, and leave with them? Sounds simple enough."

"Not exactly," Elora replied, a smile tugging at her lips despite the gravity of the situation. "Each jewel requires a trial—a test of our courage, wisdom, and strength. If we fail, we risk not only our lives but also the potential power we seek to claim for Eryndor."

"Then we need to prepare," Lyra declared, her excitement infectious. "Let's train, learn what we can about the trials, and gather our strength. We can't afford to take this lightly."

As the fire crackled around them, Elora felt a sense of purpose solidifying within her. The weight of their *mission felt immense, but so did the hope that flickered in her heart. Together, they could achieve the impossible.*

Elora envisioned the moment they would claim the jewels—each representing a facet of the kingdom they loved so dearly. The Jewel of Fire, powerful and fierce; the Jewel of Tides, fluid and adaptable; and the Jewel of Stone, steadfast and unyielding. Each would not only amplify their strength but also symbolize the unity of their cause.

Ronan broke the silence, his expression turning serious. "What if the warlord learns of our quest? He won't sit idly by while we try to gather power."

Elora nodded, acknowledging the truth of his words. "We must be discreet. We can't afford to let him know our plans until we are ready to confront him."

Elora took a steadying breath, her expression hardening with resolve. "Alright," she said, her voice firm and unwavering. "We'll hold meetings in the village—prepare everyone for the fight while we're away."

As the evening wore on, Elora and her companions meticulously plotted their next steps, drafting plans and strategizing. They discussed the logistics of their journey, the challenges they might face, and how to prepare themselves mentally and physically for the trials ahead. Each suggestion added weight to their resolve, solidifying their commitment to the mission.

As the fire began to die down and the stars twinkled above, Elora felt a profound sense of camaraderie enveloping them. They were no longer just a princess, a thief, and a guard; they were a team, bound by a shared purpose.

"Tomorrow, we begin with the Emberheart," Elora announced as the flickering light dimmed. "We'll need to be at our best to face whatever challenges lie ahead."

Ronan nods and says, his voice resolute. "Let's make sure we're ready for anything."

XVI
INTO THE FIRE

The forest was eerily quiet, the birds and creatures retreating as if they knew what was coming. Elora felt it too. The weight of what lay ahead. She had been prepared for many things on this journey, but the first trial still loomed in her mind like a shadow.

The path before them opened into jagged, rocky terrain, and the air seemed to grow thick with heat. The wind, which had been a cool breeze before, was now hot, like the breath of some ancient, slumbering beast. They reached the edge of a cliff, and there it was. The mouth of the Cave of Flames—a gaping wound in the earth, with molten rivers running through it, glowing like blood under the sun.

Elora paused, feeling the pull of something deep inside her chest, a call she couldn't ignore. Her hand instinctively reached for the hilt of her sword, as if its weight would steady her.

"We're here," Lyra said quietly, her voice carrying the same mix of awe and apprehension.

Ronan, who had been silent until now, scanned the cave's opening. His eyes narrowed, his hand brushing the edge of his blade.

"Stay close," he said, his voice low and firm, like he was speaking to soldiers about to face an enemy. His tone left no room for argument, and Elora found comfort in it. Despite their differences, Ronan had a quiet confidence that she trusted.

They crossed the threshold together. The heat hit them in waves, almost suffocating. The air was thick with the acrid smell of sulfur, the stench of burning rock and the metallic tang of molten lava. Their feet crunched on the black stone floor, and the only sound was the hiss of flames in the distance, like some great beast breathing in the dark.

Then, a voice, low and guttural, echoed from the shadows. "Who dares enter the Cave of Flames?"

Elora's heart pounded as her eyes darted to the figure emerging from the flames. It was no mere man—its body wreathed in fire, its face obscured by shadows. Only its glowing eyes were visible, burning with an intensity that was almost blinding. The heat coming from it was unbearable, and yet, the figure stood as if it were the very embodiment of flame itself.

"We seek the Jewel of Fire," Elora said, her voice steady despite the rising pressure in her chest. "We need its power to defeat the warlord who ravages our land."

The guardian's eyes flared. "Many have sought it. Few have proven worthy. You will face three trials. Fail... and you will burn."

Ronan stepped forward, hand still on his sword. "What are the trials?"

The guardian's flame twisted and writhed. "The first trial is a test of combat," it said. Its voice crackled like fire on dry wood. "Defeat the Fire Elemental, and you may proceed."

The air vibrated with energy, and before any of them could react, the cavern trembled. A deep, guttural roar echoed from the shadows, and the ground shook beneath them. Elora's pulse raced as a massive shape began to form, rising out of the flames. The Fire Elemental—its body composed entirely of molten rock and flame—slowly emerged, its eyes like twin infernos. It let out a roar that sent heat rippling through the cavern, and the ground cracked beneath its weight.

"Get back!" Ronan yelled, pulling them all back with a sharp motion of his arm. "Stay spread out!"

The Elemental moved, its massive limbs swinging with terrifying force. Elora's instincts kicked in. She darted to the left, watching as Ronan did the same. They were quick—too quick for the Elemental's slow, lumbering movements—but that didn't make it any less dangerous. With a roar, the creature swung its flaming fist in their direction. Ronan leapt backward, narrowly avoiding it, his sword drawn in one fluid motion.

Lyra, agile as ever, rushed forward, dodging the Elemental's grasping hands with acrobatic ease. She taunted it, ducking and weaving around its fiery limbs, moving with a fluidity that made the creature's fury only grow.

Elora tightened her grip on her sword, ready to strike. "We need to find its core—where the flame is weakest!"

Ronan's eyes narrowed as he scanned the creature's chest, the fire roiling and swirling like a tempest. He didn't hesitate. "Lyra, keep it distracted!"

Lyra darted forward again, sliding beneath one of the Elemental's limbs just as it swung downward. The massive creature howled, its molten form cracking and shifting as it tried to bring its full force down on her. She rolled to the side, narrowly avoiding the searing heat of the attack.

Elora saw her chance. With Ronan moving to the left, she rushed toward the Elemental's chest, focusing on the core of its molten heart. It was pulsating, a flickering orange light beneath the surface of its fiery form.

Elora drove her blade into it with all her might, and Ronan followed with a strike of his own. There was a moment—a heartbeat—of perfect silence before the Elemental let out a thunderous scream. The flames erupted outward, showering them with molten embers. Elora threw herself back just in time, her clothes singeing at the edges.

The Elemental collapsed, its body falling apart in a shower of sparks and ash. The cavern fell silent once more.

The guardian stepped forward from the shadows, its fiery gaze glinting with what almost looked like approval. "You have proven your strength. The second trial awaits."

Elora barely had time to catch her breath before the ground beneath them trembled again. The air thickened with heat, and a wall of flame shot up, cutting them off from the path ahead. The guardian's voice rang out, calm but unyielding.

"You must traverse the Path of Flames. Fail... and you will be consumed."

Elora's chest tightened. She could feel the heat on her skin already, the oppressive weight of it pressing in on her. They had just faced the Fire Elemental, but this... this was different. This wasn't just about strength—it was about survival.

"Stay close and move quickly!" Ronan barked, his voice cutting through the rising tension.

Without waiting, he charged forward, leading the way as the flames roared higher. Elora was right behind him, Lyra moving like a shadow at their backs. They didn't have time to think—only to move.

The path was narrow, and the flames surged all around them. Every time they thought they had enough space to move, another wave of fire would shoot up, forcing them to jump or duck. The heat was unbearable, searing their skin, and the air felt thick with smoke.

Elora's vision blurred from the heat, her muscles burning from the exertion. The fire was everywhere, coming from all sides. Just as she thought she couldn't take another step, a wall of fire rose directly in front of her. She barely had time to react before it began closing in, its intensity like a furnace.

Elora's legs buckled, her breath coming in short, sharp gasps. The heat of the fire was suffocating, waves of scorching air lapping at her skin, making every movement feel like it would be her last.

"I can't..." she gasped, her legs trembling with exhaustion, muscles seizing under the strain.

Ronan was there in an instant. Without hesitation, he reached for her, pulling her against him, his body a solid wall against the searing heat. His arm wrapped tightly around her waist, holding her close. "Trust me," he muttered, his voice low and stable above the roar of the flames.

Before she could protest, he surged forward, pulling her with him, keeping her shielded in the crook of his arm as he moved through the wall of fire. The heat was unbearable, but he didn't flinch. His body blocked the worst of the flames, his cloak billowing behind them like a protective barrier.

Elora's breath hitched as the flames lashed at them. She could feel the heat searing through her, but Ronan was like an anchor, his presence grounding her. She pressed herself against him, unwilling to be lost in the inferno.

"Keep moving, Elora," Ronan grunted, his grip tightening around her as they pushed through the blaze.

The fire roared around them, hungry and relentless, but Ronan moved with purpose, his steps sure and steady. They advanced inch by inch, every second feeling like an eternity, until they broke through the worst of the flames.

Elora stumbled, but Ronan steadied her, pushing her toward the relative safety of the other side. The air was still hot, but not nearly as oppressive.

Lyra wasn't far behind them. She darted through the flames with an almost unnatural grace, her movements fluid and precise, every leap and twist taking her out of harm's way. The fire seemed to avoid her, her agility allowing her to dance through the inferno like a shadow.

As Elora caught her breath, she glanced over at Lyra. "You make it look easy," she said, a weak smile on her lips.

Lyra shot her a smirk, her eyes glittering with the thrill of the challenge. "It's all about knowing how to move with it. You're getting there," she teased.

Elora managed a chuckle, the tension of the trial loosening its grip on her. She glanced at Ronan, whose expression was as impassive as ever, though the strain in his eyes didn't go unnoticed.

"Thanks," she murmured, her voice quiet but sincere.

Ronan gave a small, almost imperceptible nod. "No need to thank me. We're not done yet."

They stood for a moment, catching their breath, before the ground beneath them trembled once again, signaling that the next challenge was about to begin.

The guardian was waiting, its flames flickering in approval. "You have proven your agility. The final trial awaits."

And then, the ground shattered beneath their feet. A roaring vortex of flames spun in the center of the *cavern, and from it, a massive shape emerged—a Fire Drake, its molten body glowing like the heart of a volcano. It spread its wings wide, sending a wave of heat that made their skin crawl. Its roar shook the cavern walls.*

Elora's heart pounded. This was it—the final trial. She could feel the weight of it pressing down on her, her body aching from the earlier battle, but there was no turning back now.

Lyra was the first to react. "Distract it!" she yelled. "We'll aim for its wings!"

Ronan nodded, his face grim. "On three."

And then, like a storm, they were moving. Lyra danced between the drake's massive claws, evading its fiery attacks with a precision that left the beast enraged. Ronan and Elora rushed forward, aiming for its wings, the key to bringing it down.

The Fire Drake howled, a guttural, primal roar that echoed through the cavern, shaking the very walls. Its eyes blazed with molten fury, and with a violent snarl, it lunged at Ronan. Time seemed to slow as the beast's massive jaws opened wide, flames licking from its throat.

In an instant, it collided with Ronan, knocking him off his feet and sending him flying across the cave. His back slammed into the jagged stone wall with a sickening crack, the impact stealing the breath from his lungs. He slumped to the ground, dazed, the world spinning as the echo of the drake's roar rang in his ears.

"Ronan!" he heard her through the fog of pain, her voice sharp with panic.

Elora's boots thudded against the ground as she rushed to his side, her breath coming in ragged gasps, her eyes wide with worry. Her hand hovered over his chest, but she didn't stop to check if he was okay—not yet. There was no time for that.

"Stay with me," she muttered, eyes flickering back to the drake, which was already turning, ready to unleash another torrent of fire. "We need to strike together. We don't have long."

Ronan's head was spinning, but he could hear her. He could always hear her. Slowly, painfully, he pushed himself up, hands shaking as he used the wall for support. Elora was already on her feet, her stance unwavering, her sword held tightly in her grip. Her eyes met his, fierce and resolute.

"Ronan, get up!" Her voice was firm, but the urgency behind it was clear. "I need you. We have to take it down together."

The Fire Drake growled, its wings flapping as it turned toward them, flames gathering in its throat once more. Elora stepped in front of Ronan, positioning herself as the first line of defense, her sword raised and eyes locked on the creature. Her chest rose and fell with each breath, but there was no fear in her gaze—only the cold, burning determination of someone who would stop at nothing to protect those she cared about.

"Now, Ronan!" Elora shouted. "While it's distracted!"

Ronan, still slightly unsteady on his feet, nodded sharply, the haze of pain in his mind beginning to clear. His vision sharpened. They didn't have time for hesitation.

With a grunt, he pushed off the wall and surged forward, sword in hand. Elora was already moving, her body a blur as she closed the distance between herself and the drake. Together, they flanked it—Elora's eyes never leaving the beast as she prepared to strike.

The drake turned, its wings flapping, and for a split second, Elora saw her chance. With a swift movement, she darted in, aiming for its left wing, the blade slicing *through the air. Ronan mirrored her motion, moving to its right. They struck simultaneously—two deadly blows that drove deep into the drake's wings.*

The creature's roar was deafening as it staggered, its massive body beginning to collapse. Flames exploded from its chest in a burst of fiery fury, the heat billowing out and nearly knocking them back. The ground beneath them trembled as the drake fell, its enormous body crashing to the stone floor with a thunderous thud.

They stood there, breathing heavily, amid the wreckage of the final trial. Their bodies were scorched, their clothes singed, but they had won.

Elora glanced over at Ronan, her smirk a sharp contrast to the exhaustion in her eyes. "Took you long enough to show up."

Ronan shot her a look, a faint smile tugging at the corner of his lips despite the weight of the battle. He wiped the ash from his blade with deliberate slowness, as if savoring the moment. "I was just letting you have your fun. Didn't want to steal the spotlight."

Elora's smirk widened, but there was no teasing in her voice as she shot back, "Next time, try not to take a nap during the fight."

Ronan shot her a look, a faint smile tugging at the corner of his lips as he wiped the ash from his blade. He then straightened, giving a mock bow, his tone dripping with sarcasm. "Yes, ma'am. Wouldn't want to steal your thunder, Princess."

Elora raised an eyebrow, crossing her arms, and replies throwing his sarcasm right back at him. "Oh, don't worry, you're forgiven. Just try to keep up next time, alright?"

Lyra, breathless, rolled her eyes. "If you two are done posturing, we have a jewel to claim."

Elora chuckled, brushing soot from her shoulder, then stepped toward the pedestal, where the Jewel of Fire lay, glowing with radiant power. She reached out, her fingers brushing against its warmth.

As soon as her hand closed around it, a rush of power surged through her, igniting something deep within her. She felt the fire, not just as a force—but as part of her.

The guardian's voice rang in the air, no longer threatening, but almost respectful. "You have earned the Jewel. But remember this—it is not just power you now wield. It is responsibility."

Elora nodded, her grip tightening on the jewel. She didn't need any more reminders. She knew exactly what they had to do next. The warlord would pay for what he had done to Eryndor. This was only the beginning.

"Let's go," she said, her voice firm. "One down, two to go."

XVII
TIDES OF CHANGE

The wind carried the scent of salt and brine, a stark contrast to the dry, sun-baked air they had left behind. Elora, Ronan, and Lyra pressed onward, their steps measured and deliberate. The Jewel of Fire was secured, but the weight of the warlord's looming threat still hung over them. Every stride felt less like escape and more like an inevitable reckoning. The danger was no longer behind them. It was in front of them, waiting.

The cliffs rose unexpectedly, jagged and unyielding, like forgotten sentinels lost to time. Above them, the sky stretched wide and indifferent, while below, the ocean churned—a restless, ceaseless thing. The Temple of Tides clung to the very edge of the cliff, its shape half-wrought into the stone, as if it had been carved by the sea itself. It was not just a building; it was a wound in the earth, a scar that throbbed with the pulse of the ocean.

Lyra broke the quiet, her voice a mix of awe and something darker. "What would it be like? To bend the tide to your will?"

Elora didn't answer immediately, her eyes drawn to the temple. The sight stirred something ancient in her—a shiver of possibility, of danger. "Power's not just about bending the world to your will," she said after a long pause. "It's about understanding the rhythm of it. Knowing when to resist, when to yield."

They climbed the stone steps, the rasp of their boots lost beneath the steady crash of waves below. The temple's doors stood open, welcoming them like the maw of some unknowable creature.

Inside, the air was thick with moisture, and the scent of old salt and damp stone clung to the stone walls. Bioluminescent algae clung to the rough surfaces, casting an eerie, sickly glow. Time seemed to slow as they entered, the only sound the distant drip of water echoing through the cavernous space. A low hum thrummed through the stone, as though the temple itself was alive, waiting.

A figure emerged from the center of the pool, its form undulating, like water itself made flesh. The light seemed to bend around it, tracing the shifting lines of its body. Its eyes—dark, fathomless—met Elora's with unsettling clarity.

"You seek the Jewel of Tides," the figure's voice was soft, a murmur that seeped into their bones. "But the ocean does not give lightly."

Elora felt a tightening in her chest, a kind of inevitability that she couldn't quite shake. "What must we do to claim it?"

The figure's gaze lingered on her for a moment too long, then spoke, each word like a wave breaking on the shore. "The Trial of Water awaits. You will face the storm, the current, and the depths. To claim the jewel, you must be tested. You must be united."

Before she could respond, the waters in the pool rippled violently, pulling them toward its edge. The current grabbed Elora without warning, icy and violent, yanking her into the abyss.

Her body was swallowed by the dark, cold water, the pull of the current stronger than anything she had ever known. She flailed, but it was useless—every direction felt wrong, every breath a struggle. The world around her narrowed to dark water, stifling pressure, and an overwhelming sense of being pulled down, down, deeper than she could endure.

Her heart hammered in her chest, and memories flickered like shards of glass—her people laughing, the *warmth of their homes, the bitter sting of failure when she hadn't been enough to protect them. She sank lower, the weight of it unbearable. The past wrapped itself around her like chains, dragging her under.*

"Elora!"

Ronan's voice cut through the suffocating panic. It was steady. Present. She could feel him there, even through the chaos. She blinked, focusing, forcing her thoughts to sharpen. She could hear him. See him. His hand, an anchor in the storm.

She reached for him, her fingers brushing his, but the current tore them apart. Panic surged again, but she fought it back. Focus. Hold on.

And then, through the murk—Lyra. Her figure appeared, swift and sure, cutting through the dark like a sliver of light. The current pulled them apart again, but Elora's focus snapped into place. Stay together. Hold on.

She reached for Ronan again. This time, their hands locked.

And then, a violent roar, a wave that struck with the force of a battering ram. The world spun, her stomach lurching as water crashed over her. They were caught in it, helpless.

The whirlpool. The current swirled around them with a terrifying precision, pulling them deeper into the eye of the storm. The rush of water deafened her, the world a blur of motion. Every attempt to fight it only dragged her further into the center of the maelstrom.

"Stay together!" Lyra's voice came through the chaos—urgent, but it was quickly lost in the roar.

They fought the pull, but the whirlpool was relentless. In the swirling madness, a jagged rock appeared ahead, rising from the depths like some grotesque monument to the storm's fury. Elora's hand found it—rough, jagged, its surface cutting into her skin—but it was the only thing that would hold her steady. She clung to it with everything she had.

Then—Ronan's hand, sharp and steady, grasped her wrist, yanking her toward safety.

But before they could reach it, Lyra slammed into the rocks beside them, her body battered by the force of the water.

"Lyra!" Elora shouted, but her voice was lost to the storm.

It wasn't the current that froze her heart, but the massive shape rising from the dark.

A serpent—long, serpentine, its scales gleaming like obsidian, eyes burning with malice. Its fangs were bared, the very image of ancient hatred.

Ronan moved instantly. His blade was in his hand before Elora had time to react. "Back to back!" he shouted, already stepping forward.

The three of them moved in a frantic blur—Lyra darting to the serpent's flank, striking with a grace that bordered on reckless. The creature hissed, its attention snapping toward her. In that moment, Ronan took his shot, slashing with calculated precision. But the serpent's tail whipped out, faster than a striking arrow, and Ronan was sent crashing into the rocks, his sword skittering away.

"Ronan!" Elora's heart stopped.

Without thought, she surged forward. This wasn't just about battle anymore. This was about protecting what was left of her world, what was left of her people, what was left of them.

Heat flared in her chest as the Jewel of Fire awakened within her. She didn't think, didn't hesitate—she thrust her hand forward, unleashing the flame that had burned so brightly within her.

The fire slammed into the serpent's eye.

It shrieked, a horrible, guttural sound, its body writhing as it recoiled, retreating into the depths with a final, thunderous roar.

The water stilled. The storm quieted.

Lyra's voice trembled, as if she wasn't quite believing what had just happened. "Did we…?"

"We did," Ronan replied, his voice low, strained. He wiped the blood from his face, a grim expression settling over him, but his grip on his sword was unwavering.

Elora's hand trembled as she moved toward the pedestal. The Jewel of Tides sat there, glowing softly, its power thrumming through the air. As her fingers wrapped around it, an electric shock raced through her arm. The light flared, brilliant and searing, engulfing them in waves of blinding light.

The sound of the ocean roared in her ears.

And then—silence.

They emerged from the temple, bruised, battered, but standing. The Jewel of Tides was in their possession. The wind stung their faces, salt and fresh air tangling in their lungs. But there was no triumph in the silence now. Only something deeper. Something unfinished.

Elora turned toward the horizon, the endless stretch of ocean before them. "One more," she said, her voice steady now. The fire inside her was banked, but there was a new resolve. "Heartwood Forest. The spirits will test us there."

Lyra's smile was sharp, defiant, a promise that nothing—nothing—would break them now. "Let them try."

Ronan's hand fell on her shoulder, his gaze unreadable, but his presence solid. "We'll see it through."

Elora looked ahead, the waves crashing against the cliffs, as if daring them to move forward. One more jewel. And then, the power to end this warlord's reign.

One more.

XVIII

THE HEART OF THE EARTH

The Heartwood Forest stretched out before them, a labyrinth of towering trees and thick, tangled roots. The dense canopy above blocked most of the sunlight, casting the forest floor in an eerie twilight glow. Elora, Ronan, and Lyra moved cautiously through the undergrowth, their breaths shallow as they approached the Grove of Stone, the rumored resting place of the final jewel—Verdant's Heart. The air here was different, thick with anticipation and an ancient, primal energy. The land itself seemed to pulse beneath their feet, alive with the magic of the earth.

"Something's off," Lyra whispered, her sharp eyes scanning the shadows.

"Agreed," Ronan said, gripping the Emberheart, the fiery jewel glowing faintly in his hand. His battle-hardened senses were on high alert, every muscle in his body coiled and ready for action. "Stay sharp."

Elora remained silent, her connection to the natural world humming within her. The deeper they ventured into the forest, the more she felt it—the power of the earth, ancient and unfathomable, calling to her. Her royal lineage granted her an innate link to the magic that flowed through the land, but here, in the heart of Eryndor's untamed wilds, that connection was overwhelming.

She glanced at her companions. Ronan, ever the warrior, walked with the controlled grace of a predator, his movements precise and calculated. Beside him, Lyra, the quick-witted thief, was a coiled spring, ready to react to the slightest provocation. Each of them carried a jewel—Ronan with the Emberheart, its fiery glow illuminating his stern features, and Lyra with the Abyssal Tear, the watery jewel cool against her skin, a reminder of their past trials.

As they neared the center of the grove, the ground began to tremble beneath their feet. The air grew heavy, and the faint whisper of leaves and distant wildlife fell silent. A deep, guttural rumble echoed through the trees, and the earth split open before them with a deafening crack.

The ground shook violently as a massive fissure tore through the forest floor. From the gaping chasm, a hulking figure emerged—an enormous wolf, easily three times the size of any normal beast, its fur a tangle of vines and moss, its eyes glowing like molten gold. Its snout exhaled mist, the air around it alive with the scent of damp earth and ancient magic. This was the guardian of the Verdant's Heart, the final trial that stood between them and the jewel they sought.

The wolf let out a thunderous growl, the sound reverberating through the trees like the rumble of a distant avalanche. It locked its piercing gaze onto Elora, recognizing in her the bloodline of Aeloria—the royal connection to the natural forces that governed the land.

Before any of them could react, the jewels in Ronan and Lyra's hands pulsed with a sudden, blinding light. The energy within the Emberheart and Abyssal Tear surged forth, manifesting in the form of creatures—beasts they had faced before, reborn from the magic of the jewels.

Ronan's eyes widened as the fire creature, the one they had fought in the Cave of Flames, materialized once again, its molten body blazing with renewed fury. It roared, a river of flame spilling from its jaws as it charged toward Ronan, its fiery tendrils lashing out like whips.

Simultaneously, Lyra let out a startled gasp as the watery serpent from the Temple of Tides slithered into existence, its massive form coiling around the trees, hissing menacingly as it advanced toward her. Its scales shimmered with the dark hues of the Abyssal Tear, its eyes reflecting the ocean's depths.

"Elora, it's happening again!" Lyra shouted, her voice tinged with panic as she backed away from the serpent, her daggers raised defensively.

Ronan, already swinging his sword at the fire creature, cursed under his breath. "It's their magic! The jewels are calling them back!"

Elora's heart pounded in her chest as the realization hit her. This was their final test—a culmination of everything they had faced. Each of them would have to battle the creatures they had already conquered, alone, with no help from the others. The wolf—the final guardian—stood before her, its gaze unwavering, its muscles tense as it prepared to strike. She was on her own.

Ronan was the first to engage, his sword igniting in flames as he swung it toward the fire creature. The Emberheart in his hand pulsed with power, feeding him the strength he needed to combat the molten beast. It lunged at him, flames erupting from its claws as they clashed. Sparks flew with every strike, and the ground beneath them scorched with each step. Ronan *fought with all the precision and ferocity of a seasoned warrior, every movement a dance of death between man and fire.*

On the other side, Lyra was already darting between the trees, using her agility to stay one step ahead of the serpent's lethal strikes. The Abyssal Tear glowed faintly in her hand, allowing her to manipulate the water around her, deflecting the serpent's attacks with waves of her own. She fought with a wild grace, her daggers flashing as she struck out at the creature, aiming for its vulnerable spots between its scales.

But Elora's battle was different.

The giant wolf moved with terrifying speed for its size, charging toward her with the force of a storm. Elora barely had time to react, raising her sword to block its massive claws. The impact sent her stumbling backward, her arms shaking from the force. The wolf's growl reverberated through her bones, and she could feel the ancient magic pulsing through it—a raw, untamed power that mirrored her own.

She summoned her magic, calling upon the earth itself to aid her. Vines erupted from the ground, snaking around the wolf's legs in an attempt to bind it. But the creature was too powerful. It tore through the vines with ease, its jaws snapping dangerously close to Elora's face as she dodged another attack.

The wolf was relentless, its movements a blur of speed and strength. Elora swung her sword, aiming for its side, but the wolf was faster. It leaped out of the way and came at her again, knocking her off balance. She hit the ground hard, the air leaving her lungs in a painful gasp. Before she could get up, the wolf was on top of her, its massive paw pinning her to the ground.

"Elora!" Lyra's voice rang out, but she couldn't intervene. Neither could Ronan. The rules of the trial were clear: they had to fight their battles alone, or they would lose the chance to claim Verdant's Heart.

The wolf's growl was deafening as it bared its teeth, inches from Elora's throat. She struggled to breathe, the weight of the creature crushing her. Pain lanced through her body, and for a brief moment, she feared this was it. She was going to die here, in the heart of the forest, alone.

But something deep inside her refused to give up.

This wolf wasn't just a beast—it was part of the earth, part of the natural order. And so was she. Her royal bloodline, the magic of Aeloria, tied her to the land in ways no one else could understand. She closed her eyes, forcing herself to calm her racing heart. She reached out, not with her hands, but with her mind, searching for the connection she knew was there.

The wolf growled again, but its movements slowed, as if it, too, felt the shift in the air.

Elora whispered, her voice barely audible, "I'm not your enemy."

The wolf hesitated, its golden eyes flickering with something other than rage—curiosity, perhaps. Elora could feel the bond between them strengthening, a thread of understanding that tied her to this creature of the earth.

"I'm not here to destroy you," she continued, her voice stronger now. "I'm here to protect what you protect. We're the same."

The wolf's growl softened, its eyes searching hers as if it was weighing her words. Elora didn't move, didn't struggle. She let her magic flow through her, not as an attack, but as a connection. She could feel the heartbeat of the earth beneath her, the pulse of life that ran through the wolf, through the trees, through everything.

For a long moment, there was silence. And then, the wolf stepped back, its massive paw lifting off her chest. It stood over her, its golden eyes calm now, its growls replaced by a low, almost mournful whine.

Elora slowly got to her feet, her legs shaking beneath her. She reached out, her hand trembling, and touched the wolf's fur. It was soft, despite its wild appearance, and as her fingers brushed its side, she felt a wave of peace wash over her.

"You're not my enemy," she repeated softly. "You're my ally."

The wolf huffed softly, a sound that might have been agreement. It lowered its head in acknowledgment, and Elora felt the weight of their bond solidify. The earth had chosen her, and in turn, the wolf had accepted her.

Behind her, Ronan and Lyra stood in stunned silence. Their battles were over, their creatures defeated. But none of them had expected this—the wolf, the guardian of Verdant's Heart, now stood beside Elora, not as a foe, but as a friend.

The ground trembled once more, but this time, it wasn't a threat. From the heart of the grove, the final jewel rose from the earth, its emerald glow casting a soft light across the forest. Verdant's Heart hovered in the air, waiting to be claimed.

Elora stepped forward, her hand still resting on the wolf's side, and took the jewel.

The wolf let out a low, rumbling sound, its eyes glowing with approval. It turned and retreated into the shadows of the forest, back to its place as guardian of the grove.

Elora watched it go, a soft smile on her lips. "Thank you," she whispered.

The ground was still for the first time since they'd entered the grove, and the tension that had gripped them all finally began to fade. Elora held the Verdant's Heart in her hand, its soft green glow illuminating the grove as if the very essence of nature had been distilled into the jewel.

Ronan and Lyra approached her, both of them bruised and exhausted, but alive.

"You tamed it," Lyra said, her voice a mixture of disbelief and awe. "I've never seen anything like that."

Ronan, ever the pragmatist, sheathed his sword and looked at Elora with a small, approving nod. "You didn't just fight the earth— you became part of it."

Elora nodded, though her body still ached from the wolf's attack. The bond she had formed with the creature wasn't one of dominance, but of understanding. She had connected with the earth in a way she hadn't even known was possible.

"The wolf won't come with us," Elora said softly, watching the shadows where the creature had disappeared. "This is its home, its purpose. But we've gained an ally in this place."

Lyra grinned, though she winced as she touched a bruise on her arm. "I'll take that. Having a giant wolf watching our backs, even from afar, is not something I'm going to complain about."

They stood there for a moment longer, basking in the silence of the forest, the weight of their victory settling over them. The three jewels—Emberheart, Abyssal Tear, and Verdant's Heart—were finally in their possession. With them, they held the power to challenge the warlord, to reclaim Eryndor from his grasp.

Elora looked down at the jewel in her hand, its soft green light a symbol of the life they were fighting for. The warlord had no idea what was coming for him.

"Let's go," Elora said, her voice steady. "We have a kingdom to save."

Together, they turned and made their way out of the grove, the path ahead still dangerous, but clearer than it had ever been.

● 171 ●

The final battle awaited them.

XIX
THE WEIGHT OF POWER

In the stillness of the hidden village, the air was thick with tension. Elora stood at the center of the training ground, her fingers wrapped delicately around the Emerald Jewel. It pulsed with an ancient, steady rhythm—its green glow a heartbeat that seemed to synchronize with her own. She felt it: a raw, untamed power thrumming beneath her skin, beckoning, urging her to let it flood her senses. But with that call came a heavy weight—a responsibility she was not yet ready to shoulder.

"Focus, Elora," Ronan's voice cut through the silence, calm but insistent. He stood a few paces away, arms crossed, watching her with a mixture of concern and determination. "You have to connect with it. Let it guide you."

Elora's eyes fluttered closed as she exhaled slowly, trying to center herself. The chaos in her mind mirrored the power thrumming within her—the faces of the villagers, the cries of those who had suffered under the warlord's reign. The memories pressed down on her like an unbearable weight, every one of them urging her to act, but at what cost?

"I'm trying," she said, her voice strained. "But it feels... chaotic. Like it's alive."

"Good." Ronan's voice softened, though his gaze never wavered. "That means it recognizes you. The power is there; you just need to learn how to wield it."

Elora's gaze fixed on the Jewel in her palm. Its light flickered, casting shadows on her face, twisting her features in an ethereal, almost unsettling way. "But what if I can't control it?" she whispered, her voice trembling with doubt. "What if it controls me instead?"

Ronan's eyes softened with understanding. He took a small step closer, his gaze steady. "I won't let that happen."

The warmth of his words settled for a moment in her chest, but the fear was relentless. Elora closed her eyes again, attempting to steady her breath. She felt the jewel's energy stir within her—an electric pulse, like a river surging, begging to be released. But every instinct told her to resist it. What if it was too much? What if, in the end, it consumed her as it had consumed the warlord?

As she concentrated, the glow of the jewel intensified. Its energy surged like a wave crashing against her chest, as if testing her resolve. It was seductive, its power a sweet whisper urging her to let go, to embrace the strength it promised. She could feel the weight of the warlord's cruelty in every beat of her heart, the injustice of his reign pressing against her like a stone in her throat. She wanted to fight, to stand against it all. But at what cost?

"I can't do this," she murmured, her chest tightening. The chaos of the jewel's power felt as if it was pulling her apart. "I'm not ready."

"You are," Ronan said firmly, his voice a lifeline. He stepped forward, closer now, his presence grounding her. "You're not just a princess anymore. You're a warrior. And warriors don't wait for the world to change—they change it."

The jewel pulsed again, brighter this time, and Elora's grip tightened instinctively. The energy raced through her like wildfire, intoxicating and overwhelming. She could feel it, the raw potential. She could almost taste the power. But at what cost?

She swallowed hard, her voice strained. "What if I become like him?" she whispered. The warlord's face flashed before her mind's eye—his cold eyes, the cruelty in his every command, the way he twisted his power to dominate. "What if this power changes me? What if I lose myself in it?"

"Take a step back," Ronan said, his tone softer now, as though he knew she was teetering on the edge. "Remember, the jewel chose you. There's a reason for that."

Elora closed her eyes again, trying to remember why she had come to this place. She thought of the villagers—of their hope and their desperation. She thought of her friends, the lives they had lost, and the future they all dreamed of. The light of that hope pushed against the shadow of her doubt, like roots pushing through the dark earth. This was for them.

Slowly, she felt the pull of the jewel's power shift. The connection between them solidified—a bond forged not in fear, but in resolve. The pulsing light steadied, and the chaotic energy became less frenetic, more controlled. Elora's breath steadied, and for the first time, she didn't feel like she was fighting it. She was part of it.

"I can do this," she whispered to herself, the words more a declaration than a promise.

The energy surged again—stronger, faster, more potent than before. Elora's heartbeat quickened, but this time, she welcomed the rush. She felt the surge of power flood her veins, a river of strength that coursed through her, awakening something deep inside. She could feel the earth beneath her feet, the wind in the air, every living thing around her, connected through the energy the jewel shared.

But then, it happened. The energy snapped, erratic—wild. The power twisted, veering out of control. Elora gasped as her vision blurred, the force pulling her in multiple directions at once. She could hear voices now, distant whispers, urging her to let go.

Embrace me, Elora... together, we will be unstoppable.

"NO!" she cried out, her voice raw as the words tried to slip from her lips. She shook her head, desperately fighting the seductive pull. Memories of the warlord's tyranny flooded her mind, the pain, the fear. His power had come from submission, from dominance. Not from connection.

With a final, defiant shout, she reached deep within herself, searching for the strength to resist. This was not the way. She was not him. She would never be him.

The jewel's light flared one last time, then abruptly dimmed, settling back into a soft, rhythmic pulse. Elora collapsed to her knees, breathing heavily, her chest rising and falling as she tried to steady her racing heart. She glanced at the jewel in her hand, its glow steady now—a reminder of both her strength and her struggle.

"Elora!" Ronan's voice rang out, sharp with worry as he rushed to her side. He knelt beside her, his hands hovering near her, unsure whether to touch or not.

"I'm… fine," she panted, wiping the sweat from her brow. "Just a little overwhelmed."

"That was intense," he said, his voice tinged with awe. "You were so close. It was—" He stopped himself, taking a breath, then placed a hand on her shoulder. "You're stronger than you realize. You resisted it."

Elora's fingers trembled around the jewel. She could still feel its power thrumming beneath her skin, beckoning her to try again. But the fear still lingered—what if next time, she couldn't control it? What if it took her?

"I won't let it take me," she whispered, more to herself than to Ronan. "I can't let it."

"You won't," he said with a quiet certainty, looking at her with the kind of resolve she hadn't seen in a long time. "You've already shown that you can resist it. And that's just the beginning."

She nodded, taking a deep breath. With Ronan beside her, she felt steadier. The path ahead was still uncertain, but for the first time, she felt a flicker of hope—a flame against the darkness.

"We'll train again tomorrow," she said, rising to her feet, the jewel pulsing softly in her palm. "And we'll learn to use this power. Not just for me—for all of Eryndor."

Ronan smiled, his expression softening with pride. "Together, we'll master it. And together, we'll take down the warlord."

As they turned toward the village, the last light of the setting sun cast long shadows across the training ground, the world bathed in the soft glow of possibility. The night stretched before them—a future both uncertain and filled with hope.

And Elora knew that no matter what came, she would rise to meet it.

XX

EMBRACING THE POWER

The sun hung low in the sky, casting an amber glow over the hidden village, bathing the landscape in hues of gold and orange. Elora stood in the clearing once more, her heart pounding with a mix of anxiety and anticipation. Today would be different. Today, she would confront the Emerald Jewel and learn to control its immense power once and for all.

Ronan was beside her, his presence a steady anchor against the rising tide of her nerves. "Are you ready?" he asked, his voice low and steady, laced with concern. His eyes searched hers, seeking reassurance.

Elora took a deep breath, allowing the air to fill her lungs, steadying her racing heart. "I have to be. We don't have time to waste. The warlord is gathering his forces, and we need every advantage we can get."

Determination surged within her as she squared her shoulders, her resolve sharpening. Together, they approached the clearing where the Emerald lay, its radiant glow pulsating softly in the twilight. The jewel seemed to hum with energy, responding to their presence like a living entity. Elora could feel it beckoning her, inviting her to tap into its power, whispering promises of strength and freedom.

"Remember what we talked about," Ronan said, stepping back slightly to give her space, his eyes never leaving her. "You need to find that balance. Focus on your own strength, and don't let the jewel overwhelm you."

With a determined nod, Elora crouched down and placed her hands on the cool surface of the jewel. Instantly, a wave of energy surged through her, stronger than anything she had felt before. It coursed through her veins, igniting every nerve, and for a moment, she was lost in its brilliance, enveloped by a shimmering sea of emerald light.

"Control," she whispered to herself, the mantra echoing in her mind. "I am in control."

As she concentrated, the jewel responded, its glow intensifying. Visions flickered before her eyes—memories of her journey, her struggles, and the faces of her friends who had stood by her side through thick and thin. Each image fueled her resolve, and she felt herself becoming one with the jewel, its power resonating within her like the notes of a symphony.

But just as she felt the beginnings of mastery, the familiar darkness crept in, its cold tendrils seeking to envelop her. "No!" she gasped, fighting against the pull, her voice breaking with desperation. "I won't let you take control!"

The jewel pulsed violently, as if responding to her defiance, and Elora's heart raced as the energy swirled around her, chaotic and wild. "I am not afraid!" she shouted, channeling her fear into determination, her voice echoing through the clearing. "I won't back down!"

With a surge of willpower, she envisioned the light of the jewel merging with her own essence, two forces colliding to create something greater than either alone. "I am the master of this power!" she declared, her voice steady and fierce, resounding like a battle cry. "I will not be your vessel!"

The energy shuddered around her, and Elora felt the tumult within her begin to stabilize. Slowly, she found her rhythm, drawing strength from the jewel while maintaining her own identity. She focused on the warmth that spread through her, banishing the cold *tendrils of darkness that sought to take over.*

As the power aligned with her spirit, a brilliant light erupted from the Emerald, enveloping her in a cocoon of radiant energy. She gasped, the sensation exhilarating yet overwhelming. The jewel's essence flowed into her, enhancing her abilities, sharpening her instincts, heightening her senses.

Then, the final transformation came.

Her eyes flared to life, turning an otherworldly, godly white. A light so bright it seemed to shimmer with the very essence of the heavens themselves. It was the sign of a new bearer—the moment she fully embraced the Jewel's power, the moment the Emerald chose her as its rightful vessel, after decades of waiting. She felt the ancient power surge through her, binding her to the very core of the Jewel, now an inseparable part of her.

"Elora…" Ronan's voice trembled as he stared at her. His face was filled with awe and something else—concern, maybe fear. "Your eyes…"

Elora barely heard him. The world around her had faded into the background. All she felt, all she knew, was the power coursing through her, the Jewel's strength now a part of her very essence. She was no longer just Elora, princess of Eryndor. She was the new bearer of the Emerald Jewel's power—a force unlike any the world had seen in decades.

"I am Elora," she spoke, her voice now resonating with an echo that seemed to stretch beyond time itself. "I am the master of this power. I will never be controlled."

Her voice echoed with finality, as if the Jewel itself spoke through her. It had accepted her.

The light around her swirled, a radiant cyclone, as the Jewel's energy intensified. The clearing became a sea of emerald brilliance, the light radiating outward in every direction. Elora—her form now glowing with the pure essence of the Jewel—stood at the center, a force of nature, her eyes blazing white like twin stars in the night sky.

With a fierce cry, she sent a wave of energy outwards—a burst of light that sent ripples through the air. The ground beneath her trembled, and the light seemed to push back the shadows of the forest. She was invincible now—a living manifestation of the Jewel's ancient power.

Then, as the light began to fade, her eyes returned to their normal color. The blinding brilliance dimmed, but the pulse of the Jewel's power was still within her, a quiet but undeniable presence.

Ronan, still standing a few paces away, slowly approached, his voice filled with awe and concern. "Elora, that was... incredible. But... your eyes. What happened to you?"

Elora's breath slowed, her chest rising and falling with the weight of the transformation she had just undergone. She looked at him, the intensity of her gaze still carrying the afterglow of the power within her. "It wasn't just the Jewel's power. It was me choosing to accept it. To become it."

She took a step toward him, her posture more confident than it had ever been. "I'm not the same person I was before, Ronan. This power—it doesn't control me anymore. I control it. I am its new master."

Ronan's expression was one of concern, mixed with awe. "Elora, you can't possibly know what you're dealing with. The power you just wielded—it's not just a weapon, it's a force. You're not just a princess anymore. You're something more."

Elora smiled, the weight of her words hanging in the air. "I know. And I won't let it consume me. I've embraced it fully, and now, we fight for Eryndor."

Ronan stood in silence for a moment, then nodded, though his brow remained furrowed. "You're right. And together, we'll make sure it's used for the right *reasons.*"

With that, the two of them turned, side by side, toward the village. The power of the Jewel still simmered within her, but it was a quiet force now, an ally, not a danger. They had more to do, more to learn—but Elora, now fully in command of the Jewel's strength, was ready for whatever lay ahead.

XXI

A STAND FOR ERYNDOR

The sun hung low in the sky, casting long shadows over Eryndor as Elora surveyed the village from the crest of a hill. The landscape, once vibrant and full of life, now bore the scars of looming conflict. She could see the worry etched on the faces of her people, their eyes filled with uncertainty about the coming storm. But amidst the fear, a flicker of hope ignited within her, fueled by the resilience of the villagers and the power of the jewels that hung around her neck.

"Elora!" Ronan called, his voice breaking through her thoughts. He and Lyra hurried up the hill, determination evident in their strides. "What's the plan?"

She turned to them, her heart steady with purpose. "We need to prepare the village. Every adult must learn to fight, and we have to create safe spaces for the children. If we're going to face the warlord, we need every ounce of strength we can muster."

Ronan nodded, his expression serious. "And we'll need weapons. The villagers should be armed and ready."

Lyra stepped closer, her keen eyes glinting with excitement. "I can help gather the craftsmen. We can forge new weapons, sharpen the old ones. The blacksmiths will work day and night if we can rally them."

Elora's mind raced with ideas, her vision expanding as she spoke. "Yes! We can turn the workshops into makeshift forges. We'll need every capable hand working together. And we can use the tunnels beneath the village to create hiding spots for the children. They'll be safer there."

Ronan's brow furrowed in thought. "That might buy us time, but we need to ensure the adults are ready to defend them too."

"Exactly," Elora replied, a determined gleam in her eyes. "I'll lead the training sessions. We can teach them how to use the weapons and defend themselves. It's time we empower our people."

As they set their plan into motion, Elora felt the gravity of their task weighing on her shoulders, yet a surge of adrenaline coursed through her veins. They descended the hill together, the village bustling with energy as word of Elora's resolve spread like wildfire. Villagers began to gather, their curiosity piqued.

"Listen up!" Elora called, her voice cutting through the murmurs. "We stand on the brink of war, but we will not face it as victims. We will rise as a united force! We need every able hand, every brave heart, to fight for our home!"

The crowd's eyes widened, a mixture of fear and hope reflected in their gazes. Elora continued, her voice steady and strong. "We'll be forging weapons, teaching you how to fight, and creating safe havens for our children. Together, we can defend Eryndor!"

The villagers exchanged glances, and then a murmur of agreement began to ripple through the crowd. A man stepped forward, his face lined with age but his spirit unbroken. "I'll help with the forges. I may be old, but my hands still know their craft."

Elora smiled, the man's words igniting a fire within her. "Thank you. We'll need all the skill we can muster."

As the crowd rallied, Ronan and Lyra moved to organize the villagers into groups. Elora felt the energy shift, a palpable determination settling over them. She watched as men and women began to gather tools and materials, a sense of purpose washing over the village.

Days passed like a blur, *each sunrise marking a new phase in their preparations. The sounds of clanging metal filled the air as craftsmen worked tirelessly, sparks flying from the anvils like fireflies dancing in the twilight. Elora wandered through the workshop, her heart swelling with pride as she witnessed the villagers embracing their roles.*

She stopped at the forge, where a group of blacksmiths hammered away, their muscles straining with each strike. They were transforming raw iron into weapons—swords, shields, and spears that would soon be wielded by the brave souls of Eryndor. Elora picked up a newly forged sword, its blade gleaming in the dim light. It felt heavy in her hands, a reminder of the weight of their impending fight.

"Perfectly balanced," she remarked, turning to the blacksmith. "You've outdone yourself."

The blacksmith wiped sweat from his brow, a proud grin spreading across his face. "We're all in this together, my lady. Each swing of the hammer is a swing against the warlord's tyranny."

"Exactly" Elora replied, feeling the fire of their unity ignite her spirit. "And we will forge our destiny."

Elsewhere in the village, Ronan and Lyra were *leading the training sessions. Elora made her way to the training grounds, where a mix of farmers, artisans, and townsfolk stood in a makeshift circle, their expressions a blend of anxiety and determination.*

"Alright, everyone," Ronan called, his voice steady. "We may not be soldiers, but we are fighting for our home. Elora will show you the basics of combat, and we'll work on your confidence and strength."

Elora stepped forward, her presence commanding yet encouraging. "Fighting isn't just about strength; it's about strategy and heart. Trust in yourselves, and you will find the warrior within."

The villagers began to train, their movements initially clumsy but gradually growing more confident as Elora guided them. She demonstrated techniques, her own body moving fluidly as she shared her knowledge. With each practice swing, the villagers transformed from uncertain civilians into determined defenders of their home.

As twilight descended, Elora and her friends gathered in the village square, exhaustion painted across their faces. They watched as the last rays of sunlight dipped below the horizon, a fiery sunset that mirrored the flames of their resolve.

"We've done everything we can," Lyra said, her voice a mixture of fatigue and triumph. "The villagers are ready."

Ronan nodded, his brow furrowed with thought. "But we need to stay vigilant. The warlord will not take kindly to our preparations."

Elora gazed up at the stars beginning to twinkle in the darkening sky. "We must stand strong, no matter the cost. Eryndor will not fall while we breathe."

With that promise echoing in their hearts, they turned their gazes toward the horizon, ready to face whatever awaited them. Elora felt the weight of responsibility settling on her shoulders, but she also felt a surge of strength from the people around her. Together, they were more than just a village; they were a force that would rise against the shadows threatening their home.

XXII

FINAL
CONFONTATION (I)

The first rays of dawn sliced through the horizon, scattering fiery hues of crimson and gold across the sky—each streak a shard of hope for the people of Eryndor. Elora stood at the crest of the hill, feeling the weight of what was to come. The earth beneath her feet was damp with dew, the coolness of it stark against the warmth of her pulse. She could hear the heavy beat of her heart, matching the rhythm of the land around her.

Behind her, the villagers—farmers, blacksmiths, artisans, and children—stood ready. They were not warriors. But today, they would become something more. Today, they would reclaim their home.

Elora's fingers brushed over the jewels that hung from her neck—the Emberheart, Abyssal Tear, and Verdant Heart. Each stone pulsed with ancient power, a quiet hum that reverberated deep within her. These jewels were her birthright, her responsibility. Together, they were the key to Eryndor's survival.

"Listen closely," Ronan's voice rang out, steady and commanding, cutting through the tension in the air. His eyes burned with the same fiery spirit that had fueled him from the start. "Today, we fight not just for survival, but for our families, our future. For too long, we've suffered under the warlord's tyranny. It's time to take back our land!"

Elora turned her gaze toward the horizon as the ground beneath them trembled. Hoofbeats thundered across the valley, the enemy's forces cresting the hill. The banners of the warlord fluttered darkly in the wind, and with them, a palpable sense of dread. They were close now.

Elora tightened her grip around the jewels. The heat of the Ruby of Fire stirred inside her, the red stone flaring with a deep, burning power. She could feel it rise in her chest. This is it.

"Together," she called, raising her hand high, her voice unwavering. "We will unleash the true power of Eryndor."

The villagers responded with a roar, their collective will igniting like a spark catching fire. They were ready. She could feel their strength merging with her own, a bond stronger than any weapon.

And then, the warlord's army broke over the hill. A flood of soldiers in dark armor, their faces masked in shadow, like the storm clouds that now loomed over the battlefield. Elora's heart clenched. The battle had begun.

"Let's show them the strength of our unity!" Ronan shouted, sword in hand. Lyra, at his side, her daggers gleaming in the light, nodded at Elora with a fierce smile.

Though the jewels were Elora's to wield, Ronan and Lyra were no less formidable. Together, they would stand strong.

With a roar, the battle erupted.

Elora's senses sharpened, her focus laser-precise. The Emberheart burned within her, and she raised her hands to the sky. Flames shot forth, brilliant and blinding, cascading down the hillside in waves of fire that consumed the grass and choked the air with heat. The soldiers of the warlord stumbled, faltering in the face of the inferno that Elora conjured.

But it was not enough. The warlord's forces pressed on.

Ronan, his sword a blur of silver, cut down soldiers with a precision born of years of training. Lyra, her movements a deadly dance, slipped through the chaos, her daggers flashing as she disarmed, disabled, and disoriented the enemy.

Elora, seeing the advance of the enemy still unbroken, called on the Abyssal Tear. With a wordless command, the air shimmered, thick with moisture. Water erupted from the ground, a roaring wave that crashed into the warlord's forces. Soldiers were swept off their feet, thrown into the mud as torrents of water surged through their ranks.

But as she watched the chaos unfold, Elora's gaze was drawn to something far darker: the warlord himself. He stood at the front lines, his figure cloaked in shadow, his presence suffocating, like the weight of a thousand nightmares pressing down on her. He was waiting for them.

With a cold, commanding gesture, the warlord raised his hands. The ground quaked. From the earth itself, shadowy forms began to crawl—dark, twisted, like living nightmares. Monsters born of pure malice. Elora felt her blood turn to ice.

"You think you can defeat me, girl?" The warlord's voice boomed across the battlefield, deep and sinister. "Your jewels are nothing compared to the power I wield. You fight with fire, water, and earth—tools of the light. But I am darkness incarnate!"

Elora's pulse quickened. The shadows clawed their way toward her, a tidal wave of darkness rising from the ground. The warlord was powerful. She could feel it. But I have the jewels. I have the power to stop him.

She focused, calling on the Verdant Heart—the green jewel that pulsed with the life force of the land. "Verdantia!" she cried, her voice steady despite the fear coiling in her chest.

Roots and vines burst from the ground, twisting together into thick barriers of stone and wood. The shadows slammed against them, but Elora held firm, pushing the earth to fight back.

But the warlord's laughter echoed, cruel and mocking. "You cannot hope to win, Elora. My darkness will *swallow your light. You are nothing compared to me."*

His words chilled her to the bone. She focused harder, drawing the strength of the earth beneath her, willing the Verdant Heart to work faster, to hold back the encroaching darkness. But as she did, something shifted—a sudden, suffocating pressure pressing against her mind, a tug at the core of her very being.

Then, she felt it.

A dark presence, deeper than anything she had ever known, seeping into her thoughts, swirling through her senses like an invasive shadow. No... Her hands shook, the power of the jewels in her grip faltering for a moment. It was as if the very magic she commanded had been... corrupted.

The warlord's voice cut through her thoughts, triumphant and mocking. "Did you think you were the only one with power, girl? You are mine now. I have already claimed your soul."

Elora gasped, her eyes widening in horror as the pull deepened. She felt her body grow cold, the air around her warping as the warlord's dark magic wrapped around her like a suffocating cloak.

"No," she whispered, the words barely leaving her lips. She shook her head, trying to break free of the dark grip tightening around her.

The ground trembled beneath her feet as the warlord's power surged once more. The shadows advanced, slipping through cracks in the earth, consuming everything in their path.

And then, with a sickening lurch, the world around her seemed to unravel.

The last thing Elora saw was the warlord's figure, standing taller than ever, his eyes gleaming with dark victory as the shadows consumed her mind. The jewels around her neck flickered with an unnatural, sickly glow.

And then, all went dark.

XXIII

FINAL CONFONTATION (II)

Elora's heart pounded in her chest, each beat like a drum of war. The battlefield around her had fallen silent, the screams and clashing of weapons replaced by an oppressive, suffocating stillness.

In front of her, the warlord's magic had ensnared Ronan and Lyra. His dark tendrils wrapped around their bodies, twisting and squeezing as though the very air was choking the life from them. Ronan's sword arm hung limp at his side, his face contorted in pain. Lyra, usually quick and fierce, was slumped on her knees, her eyes wide in terror, as if the warlord's dark presence had drained all her will to fight.

"You think you can defy me, child?" The warlord's voice slithered into Elora's mind, cold and taunting. "You *think you can play hero, stand against me with your puny powers? You are nothing. And your friends... They will pay the price for your stubbornness."*

Ronan gasped, his breath labored, as the warlord's dark magic seemed to choke the life from him. "Elora," he coughed, eyes wide in desperation. "Don't... don't let him—"

Lyra's voice was barely a whisper, her face pale as she locked eyes with Elora. "Please... save us."

The warlord's cold laugh echoed through the air, an awful sound that made Elora's blood run cold. His form, cloaked in shadow, loomed tall and dark before her. He stepped forward, relishing the moment, as if savoring her fear.

"You have no idea how helpless you are. You have no idea how much power I possess. You think you can defeat me with a few toys, a few trinkets of magic? You think your little rebellion stands a chance?" He flicked his hand, and the shadows binding Ronan and Lyra tightened. Ronan gasped, his breath cutting short, while Lyra's body convulsed as though she were fighting to breathe.

Elora's throat tightened with panic. No, no, no! Her heart was hammering in her chest, the weight of her failure pressing down on her. Her closest friends were dying before her eyes, helpless. This is it. This is how it ends.

"Let them go!" Elora shouted, stepping forward, the words coming from a place of desperation. "You want me? Fine. Take me. Let them go."

The warlord's eyes glinted with amusement. "You truly believe I care for your pathetic life?" He raised his hand, sending a fresh wave of dark magic that ripped through the air, causing Elora to stagger back. The surge of magic hit her like a battering ram, knocking the breath from her lungs. "You are nothing compared to me. But if you wish to beg for their lives, by all means..."

His laughter turned into a growl. "Suffer with them, Elora. You will watch them die, and you will be powerless to stop it."

Her vision blurred. She could hear Ronan and Lyra gasping, their voices straining with agony. The warlord's magic surged again, and Elora felt a sickening twist in her gut. I can't lose them. I can't lose them.

Elora's knees buckled. The jewels around her neck—her only hope—felt cold against her skin, like stones of forgotten power. The Emberheart, the Abyssal Tear, and the Verdant Heart—what were they worth now?

They pulsed weakly, their once-glowing energies flickering, as if they too were losing their will.

The warlord was right. She was just a girl, no match for him, no match for this darkness. Her body trembled with a cold that had nothing to do with the magic.

And then—

A feeling—a force—ripped through her.

"No."

Elora's heart thundered in her chest as the world around her blurred, fading into the background. Everything that had come before—the battle, the pain, the fear—seemed to fall away, leaving only the raw, unrelenting power that coursed through her veins. A surge of energy fierce and ancient swept through her, igniting her soul.

The combined strength of the jewels.

The Emberheart, the Abyssal Tear, and the Verdant Heart—three stones of immeasurable power, each pulsing with its unique rhythm. The fire, the water, and the earth—each one a part of her, but no longer separate. They were united within her, like the heartbeats of a single body.

This is what I was meant for.

•

She could feel it—the fire of the Emberheart, its heat swirling through her like a roaring inferno. The current of the Abyssal Tear, flowing cool and unstoppable like the deep oceans. The grounded strength of the Verdant Heart, its roots reaching deep into the earth, steady and unyielding.

They weren't just jewels. They were her.

Her entire body vibrated with their combined power, a force so overwhelming that it shattered her doubt, her fear, every hesitation that had once threatened to pull her under. She wasn't alone. Ronan. Lyra. Eryndor.

The people she loved, the land she fought to protect—they were depending on her.

Elora stood, her breath steady now, the fear melting away as her resolve solidified. She felt the world around her tremble with the force of the magic that surged through her.

"Get away from them!" she roared, her voice ringing out with divine authority. The words were no longer

just her own; they carried the weight of the elements themselves.

The warlord's smirk twisted into something darker. "You're too late, child. They're already mine." His dark magic tightened its grip around Ronan and Lyra, squeezing the life from them, making their bodies jerk and writhe in agony. His voice oozed with cruel satisfaction. "And soon, you will be too."

But Elora wasn't afraid. Her gaze blazed with an intensity that could have burned the very air between them. The power of the jewels filled her, flooded her with a divine energy she had never known. Her eyes—those once mortal eyes—had gone completely white, radiating a light so pure, so blinding, that it pushed the shadows back.

"No." Her voice rang out, more forceful than ever. It was no longer just Elora speaking. The power of the jewels, the voice of Eryndor itself, spoke through her now—a divine command that could not be ignored.

The warlord's confident smirk faltered, just for a moment, his eyes narrowing in realization. Elora raised her hand, the light from her body expanding outward in a wave, each jewel glowing brighter, amplifying her power. The very earth beneath her feet hummed with a resonance, as if it were echoing her power.

"By the power of Eryndor, by the strength of the earth and sky, I banish you."

With a cry that shook the heavens, Elora unleashed the full force of the jewels. A massive beam of light erupted from her palm, searing through the air like a bolt of pure, unrelenting energy. The radiance was so intense that the very landscape seemed to fade in its presence, the world turning to white as the beam shot toward the warlord with the fury of a thousand storms.

The light collided with the warlord's dark magic, a violent crash of elemental forces. The very air trembled. For a heartbeat, time stood still.

The warlord's eyes widened, his smirk vanishing into a scream of agony. His body twisted and convulsed as the light tore through him. The shadows around him shattered, his form disintegrating into the brilliance of the jewels' power. His scream was unlike anything human, an unearthly howl that sent ripples of terror across the battlefield as his dark magic was obliterated, his form crumbling into nothingness.

For a moment, all that remained was the sound of Elora's ragged breathing and the distant crash of the final remnants of battle. The ground beneath her feet seemed to sigh in relief, the air clearing as if a great weight had been lifted from the world.

The warlord was gone. The darkness had lifted.

Elora stood, her knees nearly buckling under the strain of the immense power she had just unleashed. Her chest heaved as the last remnants of light faded from her eyes, her vision returning to normal. The weight of the moment hit her like a crashing wave, and she nearly collapsed, but she held herself up. Her friends—Ronan, Lyra—were still alive. They were free.

She turned her gaze toward them, her heart in her throat. Ronan and Lyra were on their knees, gasping for air, but alive. The dark magic that had been choking them was gone, and they were free.

Without a word, Elora rushed to them, dropping to her knees beside Ronan first. He reached for her hand, his touch weak but steady.

"Elora..." His voice was hoarse, his breath shallow, but his eyes were filled with relief. "You... you did it."

Elora's heart soared. She wanted to say something—anything—but the words caught in her throat. Instead, she pulled him into a tight embrace, holding him close, her eyes welling with tears of relief.

Lyra, still catching her breath, managed a grin. "You're really something, Elora," she said, her voice laced with exhaustion but tinged with awe. "Could've done with a bit of warning, though, next time. Maybe give us a heads-up before you make the sun explode."

Lyra, still catching her breath, managed a grin. "You're really something, Elora," she said, her voice laced with exhaustion but tinged with awe. "Could've done with a bit of warning, though, next time. Maybe give us a heads-up before you make the sun explode."

Elora's chest tightened at the sight of Lyra—her fierce, loyal friend—alive, and standing. Elora didn't know what she'd expected when she unleashed that power, but it certainly hadn't been to see her friends in such a state of fragility. The tension melted from her shoulders, and without thinking, she pulled Lyra into a tight embrace, pressing her cheek to her friend's damp hair.

"I'm so sorry, Lyra," Elora whispered, her voice trembling. "I was so scared I might lose you."

Lyra's arms wrapped around her, and she could feel the weight of the battles they had fought, both physical and emotional, lifting in this simple moment. "I knew you'd save us," Lyra replied quietly, her voice muffled against Elora's shoulder. "I always knew."

As Elora pulled away from Lyra her eyes found Ronan. The sight of him—still standing, still alive—had her heart tightening in ways she hadn't expected. The fear that had gripped her when the warlord had nearly taken his life came rushing back.

Her feet moved before she thought about it, and suddenly, she was crossing the space between them and pulling him into a tight embrace.

Ronan stiffened for just a moment, clearly startled, but then his arms went around her instinctively. His heart beat against hers, strong and steady, as though trying to reassure her that he was still here, still alive.

"You're one to make an entrance," he muttered, his voice thick with emotion. His usual playful tone was there, but it was quieter now, tinged with something more.

Elora pulled away slightly, just enough to look up at him. Her smile was shaky, but it was genuine. "You know, I was really scared when the warlord almost—" She stopped herself, shaking her head. "I thought I was going to lose you, Ronan. I couldn't—" Her breath caught in her throat, the weight of everything still pressing down on her chest.

Ronan's expression softened immediately. "Hey, I'm not that easy to get rid of," he said, his hand finding her *shoulder and squeezing it. "I'm not going anywhere."*

Elora let out a shaky breath. "I don't know what I would've done if I lost you."

Ronan raised an eyebrow, trying to shift the mood. "You'd probably throw an epic tantrum," he teased, though his voice was softer than usual.

Elora chuckled, but it was strained. "Oh, you're one to talk," she shot back. "You really think I wasn't scared when you went and almost let that warlord take your life?"

Ronan's lips twitched at the corners. "I didn't almost let him, you know. I've got my own way of getting out of trouble," he said, though the joking tone didn't quite mask the vulnerability beneath it. "But I'll admit... when I saw your eyes... glowing like that? I was a little freaked out."

Elora raised an eyebrow. "Freaked out? You looked freaked out?" she teased. "Well, what about me? I almost burned us all down with those godly flames of mine. Not exactly what I had in mind when I imagined a happy ending."

Ronan's gaze softened, and he took a step closer. "I'll admit, that was... intense," he said, his tone quiet. "But you were incredible, Elora. I didn't think you had it in you. Those eyes—" He shook his head, still in awe. "I didn't think you'd ever really use that power. It was like watching something from another world."

Elora laughed, a little embarrassed, but she met his eyes with more seriousness than she'd ever shown before. "It's not like I can turn it off," she said, her voice a little less teasing now. "I just... I don't know what happened. The power... it took over. And when I saw you there—almost gone—I just couldn't let it happen."

Ronan's smile returned, though it was softer, more sincere now. "I'm glad you couldn't. You saved us, Elora. All of us."

Before Elora could say anything else, Lyra cleared her throat loudly, pulling them both from their bubble of intimacy.

"So," she began, her voice laced with sarcasm, "this is what you two are like when you're 'just friends,' huh?"

Elora froze, her heart skipping a beat. She glanced at Lyra, a flush creeping up her neck. "Lyra, don't—"

But Lyra just smirked, her arms crossed. "What? I'm just saying. I've been watching the 'just friends' act for a while now." Her gaze flicked between Elora and

Ronan, then back to Elora. "It's pretty obvious, you know."

Ronan turned to her, eyes narrowing playfully. "What do you mean, obvious?" he asked, though there was an edge of wariness in his voice.

Lyra's grin widened, sharp and knowing. "Oh, nothing," she said airily. "Just that you two are so transparent that even the village could probably figure it out by now."

Elora's face flushed again, but she couldn't help the laugh that bubbled up. "You're insufferable, you know that?" she said, though the smile tugging at her lips betrayed her.

Lyra's smirk turned into a full grin. "Takes one to know one," she shot back, her tone teasing.

Ronan was looking between them, clearly trying to deflect the conversation. "I didn't think you were so interested in us, Lyra," he said, but his words lacked their usual bravado. There was something almost... affectionate behind them.

Lyra shrugged, unfazed. "I've spent enough time with you two. It's hard not to notice," she said with a wink. "Besides, I'm starting to think I'm not the only one who knows what's really going on here."

Elora opened her mouth to protest, but she stopped herself. Instead, she let out a defeated sigh and glanced at Ronan, who was still grinning sheepishly.

"I swear," she muttered, "you're both impossible."

Lyra took a step forward, nudging Elora with her shoulder. "Yeah, and you love it."

Ronan laughed and turned to Elora, his grin turning teasing once more. "See? At least one of us knows the truth."

"Alright, alright," she said with a sigh and pulls away from Ronan, though she was still smiling. "Enough of this. We've got a whole village to rebuild."

Lyra and Ronan nodded in agreement, but their smiles lingered—genuine, unspoken. There was no need for further words. They were a team, in every sense of the word, and they'd see this through—together.

As they walked off, side by side, the sun finally breaking through the clouds, Elora felt something shift. She didn't know what the future held, or where her feelings for Ronan would go, but for now, that *didn't matter.*

They had already won.

XXIV

THE RECKONING OF BLOOD

The battlefield, now littered with the remnants of war, was still. The air buzzed with the aftershocks of magic, the tension of triumph hanging like a heavy mist. Elora stood in the center of it all, her pulse still racing from the raw force of her victory over the warlord. Her body felt both light and heavy—alive with the power she had unleashed, yet burdened by the enormity of what had just happened.

Victory should have felt sweeter. But the taste of it was bittersweet, and a gnawing unease crept into her chest.

A distant clamor broke her reverie. Hooves pounding against the earth, voices shouting her name, carried through the ruins. She recognized the familiar cadence of royal horses.

Her parents had arrived.

Elora's breath caught in her throat. She didn't know what she expected—perhaps relief or pride—but all she felt was the suffocating weight of their impending judgment.

At the front of the cavalry rode her mother, Queen Seraphine, her posture regal but her expression strained, a mixture of disbelief and concern clouding her features. King Aldrin followed closely behind, his face drawn tight with the kind of solemnity only a ruler could wear. They had come—and yet, for the first time in her life, Elora found herself wishing they hadn't.

"Elora!" her mother called, her voice sharp, filled with urgency. She dismounted swiftly, her eyes scanning her daughter, searching for signs of injury. "What have you done?"

Elora's heart tightened. "I fought for Eryndor. For our people. What else should I have done?"

"You've put yourself at risk!" her father barked, his tone uncharacteristically harsh. "What if you had gotten hurt?! What were you thinking, fighting a warlord—alone?"

The weight of his words hit her harder than she expected. "Alone? I wasn't alone. I was with my people, with my friends, fighting for something that matters. For them. For all of us."

Her father's mouth set into a grim line. "You don't understand what leadership requires, Elora. This reckless behavior undermines everything we've tried to build."

Ronan stood a few paces behind her, his arms crossed, watching the exchange quietly. He knew how hard this would be for her. The idea of confronting her parents, of standing firm against the very figures who had shaped her, was never going to be easy. But he didn't move, didn't flinch. His silence was a steady force beside her.

"You talk about leadership as if it's a throne to be inherited," Elora replied, her voice low, simmering with frustration. "You taught me that a leader must listen to their people—but I've listened, and I can't just sit idly by. People were suffering, Father. How long should've we waited? How many must die while we debate the 'right' way to lead?"

Her mother's eyes darkened with a sorrow she hadn't expected. "Do you think we didn't want to protect them? To end this war? We did what we could."

"Then it wasn't enough," Elora said, her voice rising. "If your 'protection' was so good, why were we still fighting? Why did this warlord have the power to come this close to destroying everything we've built?"

Her father flinched, the words striking deeper than he cared to admit. But instead of anger, something softer flickered in his eyes—a recognition of something he had been too blind to see before.

"Elora," he said, his tone gentler now, though still firm. "There are things you don't understand about the weight of leadership. The choices we make have consequences. Your defiance puts not only yourself at risk but the future of this kingdom."

"And staying silent," Elora shot back, "will only ensure that the future remains a reflection of the past—one of fear, stagnation, and suffering. I can't be a part of that."

Ronan stepped forward, his voice steady. "Your Majesties, Elora is right. The old ways are failing. The people need a leader who will stand with them, not from behind a throne."

Her mother's gaze flicked to him, her eyes sharp with a mother's protective instinct, but there was no mistaking the underlying recognition of truth in his words. "And how many more will need to sacrifice themselves before the message gets through? It's easy to fight when you have the power to crush your enemies, but what happens when you can't?"

Lyra, who had been silent until now, stepped forward, her voice cutting through the tension. "What happens is that you learn to fight with the people, not for them. Elora didn't act out of some blind desire for glory. She did what needed to be done."

Her mother's eyes glistened with a mixture of pride and something darker. "You always were the wild one," she murmured, shaking her head. "You're our daughter. We raised you to think before you acted."

Elora clenched her jaw, feeling the weight of her mother's disappointment settle in her chest. She had spent her life trying to live up to their expectations, to prove she could be the dutiful heir. But what if the crown they wanted her to wear no longer fit?

"Maybe the time for thinking is over," she said quietly, but with a fierce conviction. "Maybe what we need is someone willing to act. I know what's at stake now. I've seen the world we're trying to protect. If we wait for the 'right moment,' we will lose everything."

Her father's face softened, but his voice remained resolute. "The right moment is when you understand the complexities of power, Elora. When you understand that leadership isn't just about fighting; it's about keeping the kingdom together."

Elora felt her patience wear thin. "Then help me understand, because I've watched enough people suffer while we 'hold the kingdom together' through silence."

The air thickened with tension. Elora's heart pounded in her chest, but then something shifted. Her father, King Aldrin, stepped closer. "Perhaps we have been too focused on tradition. Perhaps it's time for something new."

"Fine...." Her mother, still poised, drew her sword from its sheath and held it high, its edge gleaming in the light. "Then let us forge a new beginning. One where we fight not only for power but for the people. For Eryndor."

Elora's breath caught as the weight of those words settled into her chest. They were standing with her, *at least in spirit. In the chaos of battle, in the chaos of family, she had found her truth. This was not the moment for old ways. This was the moment for new leadership, for change.*

She raised her own sword, her voice clear and strong. "For Eryndor," she cried, her voice cracking the stillness of the air.

Her people echoed her call, their voices rising like a storm. "For Eryndor!"

Ronan stood beside her, his hand resting on her shoulder—a gesture of silent support, his presence grounding. "You've got their attention," he said, a teasing grin tugging at his lips, but the warmth in his eyes spoke volumes more—a quiet, unspoken respect.

Elora shot him a glance, a glint of mischief returning to her eyes. "Wouldn't let you steal all the spotlight," she teased, her voice light but her gaze firm.

He raised an eyebrow, his smirk deepening. "You're a tough act to follow, Elora."

She shrugged, her grin widening into something that could almost be described as daring. "Someone's gotta keep things interesting."

For a beat, the words hung in the air, but the silence between them wasn't empty. It was full—of understanding, of promises yet to be spoken aloud, of a bond that went deeper than just the moment. A future, intertwined, forged in the heat of battle and the quiet moments that followed.

Before either of them could say more, Lyra's voice sliced through the air, sharp and teasing. "Took you two long enough to figure that out."

Elora shot her an exasperated look, though her lips still curled at the edges. "You really need to stop eavesdropping."

Lyra just smirked, leaning casually on her sword, her arms crossed in that way that made her seem both relaxed and entirely dangerous at the same time. "It's not my fault you two are so obvious." She paused, then turned back to the crowd with a roll of her eyes. "But fine, enough of the sappy moments. We've got a kingdom to rebuild, right, Elora? That's what you always say."

Elora chuckled softly, shaking her head, but there was no denying the fire in her eyes. "Guess someone's gotta keep Lyra grounded," she said, her voice light, but her thoughts already ahead, already on the path they'd chosen together.

The weight of their shared mission settled back into the air around them. The crowd, still waiting, seemed to hold its breath, but now there was no tension in the moment. Just the quiet certainty that, whatever came next, they would face it as one.

The villagers' cheers filled the air, their voices soaring like a chorus of hope. As Elora turned to face the future, she knew one thing for certain: this was just the beginning. The battle was over, but the real fight—for the hearts and minds of the people—was just beginning.

"Together," Elora murmured, as she looked at her parents, her friends, and the people around her, "we will rise."

And for the first time in her life, she wasn't afraid of what the future might hold.

RESOLUTION AND NEW BEGINNINGS

XXV

THE AFTERMATH

The air was thick with the bittersweet scent of victory, a sharp contrast to the devastation that lay scattered across the battlefield. Eryndor had been freed from the warlord's tyranny, but the cost of their liberation weighed heavily on Elora's heart. The sun dipped low, casting long, mournful shadows over the land that had once flourished, now scarred by battle. The kingdom itself seemed to hold its breath, suspended between grief and the faintest glimmer of hope for a future they could rebuild.

Elora stood at the edge of the battlefield, her sword hanging by her side, stained with the remnants of the fight. The cries of the fallen seemed to echo in the wind, lingering like ghosts across the soil of Eryndor. Around her, her allies moved quietly—some celebrating, their spirits buoyed by the victory, while others wore expressions of sorrow, the cost of freedom too great to ignore. The weight of what they had endured hung heavily in the air, suffocating and yet somehow uniting them all.

"Is it always like this?" Elora murmured, her voice quiet but heavy, as she turned to Ronan, who stood beside her. His arms were crossed, his face solemn yet comfortingly steady.

"What do you mean?" he asked, glancing toward the horizon, where the last rays of the sun bled into the sky.

"The victory... the aftermath. Does it always come with such a heavy price?"

Ronan nodded, his eyes scanning the ruin, his voice soft. "It often does. We fought hard to reclaim our freedom, but freedom comes with responsibility. The scars of battle run deep, both in the land and in our hearts." He hesitated for a moment before adding with a wry smile, "Though I suspect you don't know much about scars, seeing as you've got a knack for getting yourself into trouble."

Elora shot him a playful glare. "And you think you're immune to trouble? You got lucky because I was distracted back in the cave."

"Lucky?" Ronan raised an eyebrow, his grin widening. "I'd call it strategic planning. I always knew you'd need my help."

Before Elora could retort, Lyra appeared, her presence cutting through the moment like a sharp blade. Her usual fierceness was tempered with a somber understanding as she approached them, her face shadowed with unspoken grief. "We need to honor those we've lost. They gave everything for our freedom," she said quietly, her gaze distant but resolute.

Elora's chest tightened at the thought of their fallen comrades—brave souls who had fought alongside her, now lost to the chaos of war. She swallowed hard, then met Lyra's gaze. "We will honor them," she vowed. "But we must also think of the future. Eryndor is in disarray, and we need to start healing this land."

The trio stood in quiet reflection, each of them bearing the weight of the task ahead. They had fought to overthrow a tyrant, but now they faced a greater challenge: the daunting responsibility of rebuilding their kingdom. The land was scarred not only from the battle, but from years of oppression and neglect. The people needed more than just protection; they needed hope, leadership, and a vision for a future that felt distant yet possible.

As the sun dipped below the horizon, casting the battlefield in a warm, golden glow, Elora took a steadying breath and turned to her allies. "Let's gather everyone," she said, her voice steady with purpose. "We need to come together and discuss our next steps."

The three of them made their way toward the gathering of villagers, warriors, and allies. The energy in the air was palpable—exhaustion mingled with relief, but under it all was a simmering grief, the knowledge that victory had come at a steep price. The crowd—a tapestry of different faces, all linked by shared experience—stood as one, their collective hope tempered by the weight of their losses.

Elora raised her hand to call for attention. "Everyone!" she shouted, her voice rising above the murmurs of conversation. "We've fought hard for our freedom, and today, we stand on the edge of a new beginning for Eryndor. But we must not forget the sacrifices that brought us here."

A hush fell over the crowd as they turned toward her, their eyes expectant. Elora could see the exhaustion in their faces, but also the spark of something else—something she hadn't seen in them before: hope. She felt the weight of their gaze, the responsibility of leadership pressing down on her.

"We've lost many brave souls in this battle," Elora continued, her voice steady with resolve, "and we will *honor them by building a kingdom that reflects their courage and sacrifice. Eryndor must be a place where all voices are heard, and where no one has to live in fear. We owe it to those we've lost, and to ourselves."*

A murmur of agreement rippled through the crowd, the words taking root. Elora felt a surge of energy, of determination—this was the moment she had fought for. "But rebuilding will not be easy. The warlord's forces have left our land in disarray. We need to come together, to unite as one community. Each of you has something to offer—your skills, your strength, your voices."

Lyra stepped forward, her expression fierce and unyielding, but with a layer of quiet grief beneath it. "We can form committees to address the needs of the people—food, shelter, safety. We'll need volunteers to help gather resources and rebuild homes. Eryndor cannot thrive unless we all work together."

A middle-aged woman, her cheeks streaked with dirt, raised her hand from the crowd. "We have many injured and families who have lost their homes. We need to prioritize helping them."

"Yes!" Elora replied, her heart racing with the energy of the moment. "We can organize relief efforts. We'll set up temporary shelters and work together to find food for those who need it most."

The crowd burst into a flurry of discussion—voices overlapping, ideas flowing. Elora watched with a sense of awe as the people, tired but driven, began to organize themselves. They were no longer just survivors of a battle; they were a community rising from the ashes.

Days turned into weeks, and the task of rebuilding began in earnest. Elora worked tirelessly alongside her allies, moving from one location to another, coordinating efforts, and listening to the needs of the villagers. She organized teams to clear debris, rebuild homes, and establish a network of support for the displaced.

Lyra became an indispensable part of the leadership, her cunning and resourcefulness invaluable. What had once been her skill as a thief now proved essential for the rebuilding effort. She knew where to scavenge, where hidden supplies could be found, and how to make the most out of the scraps left behind. Her quick wit and determination inspired those around her, proving that even in the most chaotic moments, there was a path to resilience.

Ronan, always at Elora's side, provided the steady presence she needed. His humor, constant support, and the quiet strength he exuded helped carry her through the darkest moments. The bond between them had deepened during the battle, and now, as they worked together to rebuild, it grew even stronger.

"Honestly, Elora," Ronan teased one afternoon as they worked to clear debris, "you really think you can lead a rebuilding effort without smashing something first?"

Elora rolled her eyes, crossing her arms defiantly. "And I suppose you think you're the expert on leadership? I've seen you trip over your own feet more times than I can count."

Ronan chuckled, shaking his head. "Touché. But at least I can laugh about it. You're way too serious all the time."

"Look who's talking," Elora shot back, but a smile tugged at the corners of her lips.

Lyra, who had been listening from a nearby pile of rubble, snorted and joined in with a wry smile. "Oh please, if you two keep this up, I'm going to start charging for the entertainment."

Elora couldn't help but laugh, feeling a rare moment of lightness in the midst of everything they were facing. For a heartbeat, the weight of the world lifted.

But the challenges kept coming. Every day brought new obstacles—families struggling to find food, children wandering through the rubble, and the ever-present shadow of grief. The faces of their fallen comrades haunted her, their absence a constant reminder of what was at stake.

XXVI
REDEFINING LEADERSHIP

The sun rose over Eryndor, casting a warm glow across the kingdom. The air was fresh and crisp, tinged with the scent of earth and promise. Elora stood at the balcony of the newly reconstructed palace, gazing out over the bustling village below. The sounds of life filled her ears—the laughter of children playing, the chatter of villagers discussing plans for the day, and the rhythmic clanking of tools as people worked together to rebuild their homes.

But amid this newfound vitality, Elora felt a stirring in her heart. The battle for Eryndor's freedom had been won, yet she knew that the real challenge lay ahead. The old ways of leadership had crumbled alongside the warlord's tyranny, and now, a new vision was needed to ensure the kingdom thrived.

As she turned back into the palace, she found Ronan standing at the large wooden table in the council chamber, poring over maps and documents. His brow was furrowed in concentration, a stark contrast to the hopeful atmosphere outside. Elora approached him, her determination building with each step.

"Ronan," she said, drawing his attention. "We need to talk about the future of Eryndor."

He looked up, a flicker of interest igniting in his eyes. "What's on your mind?"

"We've fought so hard to free our people, but we can't go back to the way things were. The traditional monarchy has failed us, and we need a new system of governance—one that truly represents the voice of the people," she declared, her conviction unwavering.

Ronan's expression turned serious, his eyes narrowing in thought. "You're suggesting we create a council of representatives? It's a bold idea, Elora. But how do we ensure it works?"

Elora paced the room, her mind racing with possibilities. "We need to establish a council made up of representatives from various villages and communities across Eryndor. Each representative can voice the concerns and needs of their people, ensuring that every voice is heard. This will not just be about royal decree but about collaboration and partnership."

Ronan nodded slowly, considering her words. "It's a radical shift from how things have always been done. But maybe that's exactly what Eryndor needs—a break from tradition to foster growth."

"And you can help lead this transformation," Elora said, her gaze steady on him. "You've proven yourself as a capable leader on the battlefield, and I trust your judgment. As the Commander of the royal battalion, you'll be providing direct leadership and guidance to the soldiers within the battalion, fostering a strong sense of teamwork and discipline."

A spark of determination ignited in Ronan's eyes. "I'd be honored to take on that role. But what about you? What will your role be in this new system?"

Elora took a deep breath, feeling the weight of her responsibilities settle on her shoulders. "I want to be the shadow commander of the royal battalion—my role is primarily behind the scenes, focusing on strategy and coordination rather than being in the spotlight. I oversee the planning of operations, analyzing intelligence and assessing risks to ensure that our troops are well-prepared and that missions run smoothly.

Ronan raised an eyebrow, impressed. "That's a significant transformation. You'll have to navigate both the political landscape and the battlefield, balancing your duties to the crown and the council."

Elora nodded, her resolve firm. "I know it won't be easy, but I'm ready. The people deserve a leader who understands their struggles and champions their rights. We need to redefine what it means to lead in Eryndor."

Just then, Lyra entered the chamber, her usual mischievous grin lighting up the room. "What are you two plotting? It looks far too serious for a sunny day."

Elora smiled, grateful for Lyra's presence. "We're discussing the future of Eryndor. Ronan and I are proposing a new system of governance—a council of representatives to ensure that every voice is heard."

Lyra's eyes sparkled with intrigue. "That sounds like a brilliant idea! We can't afford to go back to the way things were. But how can I help?"

Elora exchanged glances with Ronan, a thought forming in her mind. "With your resourcefulness and skills, you'd make an excellent liaison between the council and the people. We need someone who can gather information, communicate effectively, and ensure the council stays connected to the needs of the *villages. I propose we give you the rank of Chief Liaison of Eryndor."*

Lyra beamed, her excitement palpable. "Chief Liaison? I like the sound of that! You can count on me to keep everyone informed and to represent the voices of the people."

With a newfound energy in the room, Elora felt a sense of unity take root. They were no longer just a battalion; they were a team, ready to forge a new path for their kingdom. As they continued discussing the details of the council, Elora felt hope blossom in her chest.

Over the following weeks, Elora, Ronan, and Lyra worked tirelessly to outline the structure of the new council. They organized meetings with representatives from various villages, inviting them to share their experiences and concerns. Elora was determined to ensure that the council would reflect the diverse voices of Eryndor, from farmers to artisans, warriors to scholars.

As the day of the first council meeting approached, Elora felt a mixture of excitement and trepidation. Would the people embrace this new system, or would they cling to the familiarity of the old ways? She knew that change was often met with resistance, but she believed deeply in the vision they were building.

On the day of the council meeting, Elora stood at the entrance of the grand hall, her heart pounding. She was dressed in her armor, a reminder of her commitment to the people and the battles they had fought together. The hall was filled with representatives from across Eryndor, each one buzzing with anticipation.

Ronan entered the hall beside her, his presence a steadying force. "Are you ready?" he asked, his voice low.

Elora nodded, taking a deep breath to steady her nerves. "I am. This is our moment to reshape Eryndor's future."

As they entered the hall, the murmurs quieted, and all eyes turned to them. Elora felt the weight of their gazes, a mixture of curiosity and expectation. She stepped forward, her heart racing as she began to speak.

"Welcome, everyone, to this historic council meeting. Today marks the beginning of a new era for Eryndor.

We are here to create a governance system that truly represents the voices of our people, a council where every concern is heard and every decision reflects our collective needs."

The representatives shifted in their seats, some exchanging skeptical glances. Elora pressed on, her passion igniting the room. "We have fought for our freedom, but freedom without responsibility is meaningless. We must work together to ensure that Eryndor thrives, not just survives. This council is our opportunity to shape a future where every citizen has a say in their governance."

Ronan stepped forward, his authoritative presence commanding attention. "I stand here not just as a Commander but as a fellow citizen of Eryndor. I have witnessed the strength of our people on the battlefield, and I believe that strength can translate into our governance. We have fought valiantly, and now we must work just as tirelessly to build a prosperous future for all. Together, we can protect our kingdom and ensure that the needs of our communities—education, health, and security—are prioritized."

Lyra added her voice, her enthusiasm contagious. "As the Chief Liaison of Eryndor, I am committed to ensuring that our voices resonate beyond these walls. I understand the challenges we face, but together we can amplify our voices. I will be your bridge, your communicator, and your advocate. We can't let distance or tradition silence our people; it's time to forge new paths for communication and action. Together, we will make sure that every concern is heard and every story is told."

Elora felt the energy shift in the room, the representatives leaning in as they absorbed their words. "Together, we can create a council that embodies our values—compassion, courage, and unity. Let us redefine leadership in Eryndor and build a kingdom that reflects our hopes and dreams."

A murmur of agreement rippled through the hall, and Elora felt a surge of encouragement. She could see that the representatives were beginning to envision the potential of this new system.

As the meeting continued, Elora and her allies laid out the proposed structure of the council—how representatives would be chosen, the committees that would focus on specific issues like agriculture, education, and defense, and how decisions would be made through open discussions.

The dialogue was vibrant, with representatives sharing their thoughts and concerns. Some were wary of the change, clinging to the old ways of governance, while others embraced the idea of collective decision-making. But through it all, Elora remained focused on fostering an environment of collaboration.

By the end of the meeting, Elora could feel the momentum building. The representatives were beginning to see the possibilities that lay ahead. As they discussed the details, Elora felt a sense of camaraderie grow among them, the realization that they were all in this together.

After the meeting concluded, Elora, Ronan, and Lyra gathered in a private chamber to reflect on the day's events. Elora's heart raced with exhilaration as they debriefed.

"That went better than I expected," Ronan said, a grin breaking through his earlier seriousness. "The energy in the room was electric."

Lyra nodded, her eyes sparkling. "I could feel the shift. People are ready for change; they just needed to see it was possible."

Elora smiled, her heart swelling with pride. "We've planted the seeds of a new future, and now we must nurture them. We need to continue engaging with the representatives and ensure that our vision takes root."

As the weeks turned into months, the council began to take shape. Meetings were held regularly, and representatives from all corners of Eryndor came together to discuss pressing issues, share ideas, and craft solutions.

Elora embraced her role as shadow commander, leading her warriors with unwavering determination. She worked closely with Ronan, who offered invaluable insight from his military experience. Together, they fortified Eryndor's defenses while empowering the council to make informed decisions about resource allocation and community needs.

Meanwhile, Lyra thrived in her role as Chief Liaison, traveling between villages to gather information, concerns, and hopes from the people. She became a trusted figure among the citizens, her spirited personality and keen insights ensuring that the council remained connected to the hearts of the community.

One day, while discussing plans for a new agricultural initiative, Lyra burst into the council chamber, her excitement palpable. "You won't believe what I just heard! The villagers in the eastern valley have come up with a revolutionary farming technique that could double our crop yield!"

Elora's eyes widened with interest. "Let's invite their representative to the next meeting. We need to hear their ideas and see how we can implement this across Eryndor."

As they worked to bring the representative to the next council meeting, Elora felt the weight of responsibility settle on her shoulders. The future of Eryndor was in their hands, and she was determined to honor the sacrifices made for their freedom.

Weeks turned into months, and the council flourished. Eryndor began to rebuild not only its structures but its very identity as a kingdom. The representatives grew more confident in their roles, and the citizens felt a renewed sense of hope.

But as the kingdom thrived, Elora knew that shadows still lingered. The remnants of the warlord's forces had yet to be fully eradicated, and rumors of unrest in some regions threatened to disrupt the delicate balance they had established.

One evening, as the sun dipped below the horizon, casting a golden hue over the land, Elora gathered Ronan and Lyra in the council chamber. "We need to discuss the reports of unrest in the northern villages. It seems some people are resistant to the changes we've implemented."

Ronan's expression turned serious. "We must address their concerns head-on. Ignoring them will only allow resentment to fester."

Lyra nodded, her determination unwavering. "I can go to the northern villages, speak to the people, and gather their thoughts. If they feel heard, they may be more receptive to change."

Elora's heart swelled with gratitude for her friends. "Thank you, Lyra. Your voice carries weight with the people. We must remind them that we're all in this together."

As Lyra prepared to leave for the northern villages, Elora felt a sense of hope mixed with apprehension. Change was a journey fraught with challenges, but she was determined to face them head-on.

In the days that followed, Lyra traveled to the northern villages, listening to the concerns of the people and bringing back valuable insights to the council. Through her efforts, the council was able to address the grievances, fostering a sense of collaboration and trust.

One day, during a particularly heated council meeting, tensions flared as representatives expressed their frustrations. Elora could feel the room growing tense, the weight of conflicting opinions hanging in the air.

Ronan stood, his voice cutting through the noise. "We can't lose sight of our goal. We are here to represent our people and work together for a better Eryndor. Let's remember why we're here."

Elora felt a surge of gratitude for Ronan's calm presence. "He's right. We must focus on unity, not division. If we let our disagreements overshadow our progress, we risk losing everything we've fought for."

Gradually, the representatives began to quiet, their gazes turning to Elora. "We've made incredible strides, but there will always be challenges. It's how we respond to those challenges that will define us as a council. We must listen, learn, and adapt."

As the meeting continued, Elora could feel the atmosphere shifting. The representatives began to collaborate, seeking common ground and finding solutions that honored both their individual communities and the greater good of Eryndor.

The council's transformation was a testament to their commitment to redefining leadership, and Elora knew that they were on the right path. With each passing day, they were not only rebuilding Eryndor's structures but also its very essence—one built on collaboration, respect, and shared dreams.

And as she looked out over the kingdom, Elora felt a renewed sense of hope. Eryndor was no longer just a place; it was a living, breathing entity, shaped by the voices of its people and the bonds forged in the fires of struggle.

Together, they would continue to redefine leadership, creating a future where every citizen had a stake in the kingdom's destiny.

XXVII
A NEW ERA

The sun rose over Eryndor, illuminating the kingdom in a golden glow. The air was filled with the sweet scent of blooming flowers, and the vibrant colors of the villagers' homes painted a picture of resilience and hope. Elora stood at the balcony of the palace, gazing out over the bustling village below. It had been several months since the council had been established, and in that time, Eryndor had transformed into a flourishing realm where magic and the people thrived together.

Elora had grown into her new role as the shadow commander of the royal battalion, leading with fierce determination that inspired those around her. With every passing day, she felt more confident in her leadership abilities, but she also knew the weight of responsibility that came with it. As she watched the villagers work together, rebuilding their homes and lives, she felt a surge of pride. This was a kingdom reborn—a testament to their strength and unity.

"Still staring out into the abyss, or are you just admiring your own reflection?" Ronan's voice broke through her reverie, and she turned to find him leaning against the doorframe, arms crossed and an amused smirk on his face.

"Very funny, Ronan. I'm just appreciating the view," Elora replied, rolling her eyes. "It's called leadership, something you might want to look into."

"Leadership, huh? I always thought it was just an excuse to stand around and look important," he shot back, stepping into the room.

Elora narrowed her eyes at him. "If you think this is easy, try standing up there and addressing the villagers while juggling your 'cool warrior' persona."

Ronan chuckled, his dark brown eyes glinting with mischief. "Oh, I'd be great at it. All I'd have to do is unsheathe my sword and look intimidating. You, on the other hand, have to do the talking."

Elora feigned a gasp. "And here I thought you were my loyal protector, ready to fight for our kingdom. But I see now it's all about the theatrics for you."

"Someone has to keep the audience entertained," he replied with a wink.

Elora shook her head, suppressing a smile. "Focus, Ronan. We have work to do. The first community forum is in a few days, and I want it to be perfect."

"Perfect, right. Because that's what this kingdom needs—another opportunity for people to air their grievances. What if they start asking for free food? I can see it now: 'Let's put Ronan in charge of the bread line!'" he said, his tone dripping with sarcasm.

She couldn't help but laugh. "You'd probably mess it up somehow, knowing you."

Ronan feigned offense. "Me? I have a reputation to uphold"

"Right. And that reputation is...?" Elora challenged, raising an eyebrow.

"The best swordfighter in Eryndor," he declared, puffing out his chest in mock arrogance.

Elora smirked. "Yeah whatever."

"Admit it, dont be shy, you have a liking for me, you know I'm better, " he replied crossing his arms

"I thought I was the one getting efffected by the jewels, seems like you're too. Too delusional for your own good."

Ronan just grins shaking his head accepting defeat from her verbal war

The following weeks flew by in a blur of preparations and excitement. The first community forum was scheduled, and the anticipation in the village was palpable. Elora could feel the energy in the air as she stood in the town square, surrounded by vibrant colors of banners and decorations.

Representatives from various villages gathered, each eager to voice their thoughts and concerns. As she looked out over the crowd, Elora felt a sense of pride swell within her. This was a moment she had fought for—a chance to connect with her people, to hear their stories and understand their needs.

Ronan stood beside her, arms crossed, a proud smirk on his face. "You look like you're about to face an army, not give a speech," he teased.

Elora shot him a pointed look. "Thanks for the vote of confidence, but I'll manage just fine without your *added pressure."*

Ronan shrugged, pretending to look serious. "I'm just saying, if you need backup, I'm ready to charge in at a moment's notice."

"I'll keep that in mind when I need someone to stand behind me and look good," she quipped.

The crowd erupted in applause as Elora stepped forward, addressing them with confidence. "Welcome, everyone, to our first community forum! Today, we come together to share our thoughts, ideas, and concerns for the future of Eryndor. This is your chance to speak and to be heard."

The representatives began to share their stories—tales of resilience, hope, and dreams for the future. They spoke of their struggles, their desires for better education, improved agriculture, and greater opportunities for trade.

Elora listened intently, her heart aching for their hardships but swelling with hope as they shared their visions for a better Eryndor. It was a powerful moment—a reminder of why she had fought so hard to redefine leadership in their kingdom.

At the end of the forum, Elora felt a sense of accomplishment wash over her. The people had come together, their voices resonating with a collective vision for Eryndor. As the crowd began to disperse, Ronan stepped beside her, a proud smile on his face.

"You did it, Elora. You brought the people together. This is a new era for Eryndor," he said, his tone playful yet sincere.

Elora felt a warmth spread through her chest at his words. "Thanks, but I couldn't have done it without you, Ronan. You've been a pain, but a useful one."

He laughed, shaking his head. "A useful pain? That's the best compliment I've received all day."

Just then, Lyra burst into the square, a whirlwind of energy. "Hey! Did I miss the part where Elora won over the masses and became their beloved leader?"

Elora raised an eyebrow. "Beloved? That's a bit much, don't you think?"

"Just trying to hype you up. You need a little drama in your life, Princess!" Lyra replied, winking.

"Drama? If I wanted that, I'd just challenge Ronan to another duel," Elora countered, crossing her arms.

Ronan groaned, pretending to be offended. "I'm just trying to keep the peace here, but if you insist on testing your luck, I'll gladly accept your challenge—again."

"Maybe we should just find you a cushy job in the kitchens instead," Elora suggested, a smirk on her lips.

Lyra laughed, shaking her head. "Let's not take away his fighting skills, we need him in case any more bandits show up."

"See? I'm essential," Ronan replied, feigning seriousness, earning an eye roll from Elora.

As they continued to bicker playfully, Elora felt a deepening bond forming among them. It was this camaraderie—this sense of belonging—that had become the foundation of their new Eryndor. They *were not just leaders; they were friends united in purpose*

"With A Flicker Of Magic, Eryndor Bids You Farewell...."